CW01465728

To Able
Love
SeRobi

Wicked
SECRETS

A MAFIA DUET-BOOK TWO

© 2024
Wicked Secrets
S.E. Robin

All rights reserved.

No part of this book may be used or reproduced in any manner without written permission from the authors, except in the case of brief quotations used in articles or reviews.

This book is a work of fiction. The names, characters, places, and incidents are all products of the author's imagination and are not to be construed as real. Any similarities are entirely coincidental

Editor: Magnolia Author Services
Cover Designer: Wingfield Designs
Formatter: V.R Formatting

Content warning

Intended for readers 18+

Wicked Lies and all future books within this duet are all works of fiction. Due to the nature of this duet, some content within this book may be disturbing or triggering for some readers. Reader discretion is advised.

This book is not to be used as a resource for sexual education, or as an informational guide to any sexual acts. The activities within this book are dangerous and are not meant to represent realistic expectations of sexual activity.

Found family
Gun play
He falls first
Dominant
Attempted suicide
Edging
Cock warming
Light bondage
Held captive

Adoptive siblings
Torture
Blood

If you are unsure if this book is for you please message the author on FB or instagram to find out more details.

Foreword

If you are reading this I would like to thank you for purchasing book two of a mafia duet.

I am glad you enjoyed book one and are looking forward to seeing what happens next!

I have loved being in this world and seeing it come to an end is a little sad, but who knows, we may see some of the characters again at some point ;-).

In the meantime, I hope you enjoy.

Much Love

Sarah x

PROLOGUE
Reed

I can feel the wet grass sink beneath my feet, and the damp earthy smell in the air doesn't help ease the way I feel. I'm looking around at the people gathered here today, and they're not here for Maghan. Hell, they're not even here for me! They're here for the Russo family. Carlos may have taken us in, but I'm not part of this family; not since the car "accident" that killed both him and his wife, leaving his son to take over. I've had a feeling, a bad one, that Carlos Junior had something to do with it, and ever since that day, things throughout the ranks have been shaken. Some of the older guys have "disappeared"; some are cold and hard.

Senior wouldn't stand for that. He may have been the head of one of the biggest crime families on the East side, but he was a fair man. Things have turned sinister and that's coming from me, the now-second in command.

I'm tuning in and out to the priest as he utters the age-old ashes to ashes, dust to dust... I can't listen to this shit! She was only thirteen years old, her life had barely began and what... it ends just like this? With nameless faces in the congregation acting as if they knew who she was, like they care she isn't here anymore? I don't really know how she died, only that she did. I was out of town when Carlos called to say that she'd "taken" her life and she left a note on her open laptop. *Taken her own fucking life; she was thirteen!* I feel the rage burn inside of me. Something isn't right, I can feel it in my gut, but I have no fucking proof, and each time my mind goes back to the note it makes my blood boil. My nostrils flare as I clench the fists that rest down my sides, feeling the drops of rain that start to fall from the sky. It's like the tears I can't seem to release are opening up from the heavens.

Turning, I barge into the person to my left, knocking them out of the way, and stride toward the car waiting for me. Maybe Carlos is right, there really isn't anything left for me here. Maybe taking over the operations in Italy is the best option, so I can get away from it all.

My eyes are drawn to my side, and I am pulled from the anger. Big, dark eyes stare up at me with unshed tears while small hands pull at my suit jacket, stopping me in my tracks. "What's the matter, Re Re?" asks Caitlin. I reach down and pick her up, pulling her close. "Nothing, I'm okay. I just got a little upset, but you don't need to worry about that, okay?" I try to reassure her as she rests her head on my shoulder.

Walking over to a bench, I place her on my knee. "Hey, I have to go away for a while, but I want you to know something very important and I want you to listen very, very carefully, okay?" I tell her, placing my hand under her chin and moving her so we are eye to eye. "You are perfect just the way you are. It doesn't matter what you can or cannot do, okay, you don't need to change for anyone. This Caitlin is one hundred percent perfect, and nobody else can say otherwise. Got it?" I say pointedly.

Giggling, she covers her reddening cheeks in her elbows. "Okay, Re, but I don't want you to go. Can't you stay here with me? It's my birthday next week. You'll be back for that, won't you?" She looks at me hopefully. She'll be eight years old and living with a man who has a stone for a heart.

"I'm afraid not, but I will be in touch. I promise, when you need me most, I'll be there," I tell her, placing a kiss on the top of her head. I lean into her dark hair, closing my eyes, and a knot forms in my stomach at the thought of leaving something so precious in the hands of Carlos. *I really don't know what he's capable of, but surely he won't hurt his own sister.*

Feeling a slap on my back, I look around to see him. "Look, man, the plane's fueled if you wanna go, the place is ready. There's nothing keeping you here, and we could really use you there." His lips lift in a smirk as his hand pats my shoulder again in a reassuring tap.

"I'll go. I want the paperwork for what containers we're going to be receiving, plus I want the post mortem results. They should be ready," I demand.

"All taken care of. The documents are in the SUV; you can read them on the flight," he says with a cocky smile.

"I will need to pack first. I'm happy to leave this shit; if people think I'm going to the wake, they can think again." I stand, placing Caitlin down on her feet, and feel her press into my side.

"No need, your bags are in the trunk. Everything else you need will be there." His smile spreads across his face as he turns to walk toward the waiting car. "Caitlin, come, Reed needs to leave now. Let him go," he almost spits at her.

I hope I'm making the right choice. I can't look at her as I leave. If I do, I'm never going to make it to the plane.

"Eager to get rid of me?" I scoff as I match his strides.

He turns his head to look at me. "Not at all, my friend, but I am eager to get business moving." His hand reaches for the door handle. He pulls it open and gestures for me to get in.

Without looking back, I get in the SUV and make my way to the airport to board the plane, the documents sitting heavy in my hand.

The private plane is luxurious: black leather seats with chrome trim, a bar in the corner, and as I take my seat, I am presented with a glass of champagne. I raise my eyebrow at the stewardess.

"It was preordered, sir." She looks down apologetically.

"Well, that was a misunderstanding. I'll take a vodka… neat with ice." My eyes narrow at her, and she scurries away to fix my drink.

A couple of hours later we're in the air, and I can't stand the torture of the manila envelope anymore. I rip it open in one movement and pull the contents out to read page by page.

My shoulders tense, my teeth clench, and I'm sure I'll break a molar if I don't let up soon! A noise escapes me that I don't recognize, half groan and half growl. I have no one to take the anger raging inside of me out on. Until, that is, the stewardess appears, thinking I wanted some assistance.

"Can I help you with anything, sir? " she asks.

I unbuckle my belt and stand in front of her, and she takes a step back. "You want to help? " I raise my brow in question.

Her eyes widen but she sucks in her bottom lip and slowly nods her head yes.

"Take my cock out," I demand.

Her hands quickly move to my belt and fiddle with the buckle and buttons and eventually frees me. She looks from my semi-hard cock to my eyes.

"It's not going to suck itself, sweetheart." I wink.

She drops eagerly to her knees, and I push my cock force-fully past her plump, plastic lips and fuck her mouth hard and fast. I need to release this fucking pressure I have building, and this eager slut I have at my feet is the only thing I have at hand.

Usually I find release, but her attempt at a blowjob is severely lacking and leaves a fucking lot to be desired! Pulling back, drool drips from her lips, and her bleach-blonde hair is matted from my hands pulling at it. "What's wrong?" Her watery eyes peer up at me.

"Nothing. Get up, we're done here," I say, turning my back to her and walking toward the bathroom at the back of the plane, not bothering to put my cock away as I go. It's a spacious room considering where I am, but fuck if I'm here to pick at the decor. I lean one hand against the wall above the toilet and spread my legs apart slightly, my hand gripping my cock as I use her spit to thrust back and forth until I spill my seed into the basin. *Pathetic*!

Turning toward the basin, I look at my reflection above the sink. My light blue eyes are darker--the black circles I have around my eyes aren't helping--and the usual stubble I keep has turned in to an unruly beard. I run my hands down my face, shaking my head at myself. I want to rip the suit off I'm wearing and wash off the memory of this day! Even more than that, I will never forget what I read in those documents… *Adoption certificate*! For a one and only Maghan Carter. She wasn't even my fucking sister. She knew that, and no one even thought to share that with me! I love her--*fuck*! I *loved* her. Why wouldn't she tell me?

But one thing's for fucking sure. I'm going to find out.

CHAPTER 1

Reed

10 years later

S itting on the patio with the sun warming my skin, Marco brings me my morning espresso, like clockwork, and I'm thankful for his presence here. Not that I'd let him know that, but since the start he's made the transition an easy one. He runs the house and knows what I need before I do. The old man insists on dressing in a suit even in this heat, and he prides himself on his appearance. His dark gray hair is brushed back and the lines show at the corner of his dark brown eyes. He's a kind man, one that shouldn't and doesn't deserve to be involved in our world, but he was sent here by Carlos not long after I was. He won't say anything about his past even when I pry. I mean, fuck if I *actually* give a shit. My life for the past ten years has been on a downward spiral, all because of her. My so-called sister, the one person who I ever truly loved. She's the one that's frozen my fucking heart, turned it into stone. Now I don't give a shit about myself, let alone why this kind old man is at my beck and call.

S. E. Robin

"Anything else, sir?" Marco questions, the silver tray he carries held in his fingers in front of him, reflecting the sun back into my eyes.

"You could stop carrying that fucking tray around. One day you're going to blind me, you know!" Spitting the words, I turn to look at the sparkling sea in front of me. Living in Maiori has its upsides. It's a slice of the Amalfi Coast paradise with a beautiful sandy beach, and the best part about this place is the lack of tourists. I can admire the breathtaking views of the sea and mountains without being interrupted, well apart from Marco *and* Carlos--can't fucking forget about him. His day will come. I may be fucked up the majority of the time but I know for sure the death of Maghan wasn't suicide. It can't have been, and that motherfucker has the answers I need. I just need to bide my time.

"Your, err, appointment will be here soon, sir. Shall I see her through to the main room?" His voice is a low whisper.

"Marco, she's a hooker, you don't need to whisper. I'll be ready for her when I finally get five fucking minutes of peace. And stop calling me sir--we've been over this," I state as I look at the older gentleman. He raises his bushy eyebrows at me.

"Very well. If you need anything you know where I am, si.. Reed." He nods his head as he retreats back into the villa.

Leaning forward, I reach into the pocket of my linen slacks and pull out the only thing that's kept me sane over the years, the one constant in my life that I can depend on. Holding the baggy up, I flick the white powdered contents with my right hand. *Fuck, now I could use that fucking tray*! Gripping the bag with my thumb and forefinger, I open it slightly and tip the contents on to the saucer. Using the bag, I get the best line I can. Closing my nostril with one finger, I lean forward and inhale. My finger goes to my mouth out of habit and I suck, then run it over the saucer to gather up any left over powder I may have missed and rise to my feet while my finger runs along my gums.

8

Fuck, there's nothing I love more than getting a morning hit and seeing the sun reflect off of the sea. The colors are mesmerizing. I stalk toward the villa, which is more like a mansion. It's bigger than I will ever need but that's Carlos for you, always having to be bigger and "better" than the rest. Its rustic red-tiled roof leading down to the white-washed stone walls is picturesque, and I suppose this is where you'd expect the CEO of a Fortune 500 corporation to live. It's amazing what people believe--or rather what they let themselves believe--when you're spending obscene amounts of money to use their little village to switch containers.

Making my way upstairs to my guest room, I see her. My eyes roll and I groan outwardly at the sight. Spread eagled and naked in the middle of the four poster hardwood bed is the woman who I am paying to fuck away my stresses. Her jet black hair is tangled across the stark white pillow, and her eyes follow me as I stalk toward the bed.

"Who told you to get undressed?" I snarl.

"You want to fuck, yes?" Her eyebrow raises in question.

"You don't need to be naked for me to fuck you, get dressed. Now!" I demand.

She jumps from the bed, pulling her clothes on. Her skin is pasty, her lips pumped full of plastic, just like her breasts.

"Stand facing forward with your hands against the wall," I command.

I lower my hand and start to trace the outline of my cock, who hasn't got the message that there is a naked woman in the vicinity.

"Lift your skirt and spread your legs, show me your pussy... play with yourself, make yourself nice and wet," I say as I sit on the edge of the bed, watching her follow my instructions.

My cock's not playing ball. Her moans are as fake as her tits. Normally I wouldn't give a shit, but today it's grinding my gears.

Spitting in my palm, I fist my cock, watching as her pussy remains as dry as the Sahara. Her moans get louder as she turns her head around, seductively nibbling on her bottom lip. A growl leaves me as my strokes become faster and more furious. I close my eyes, trying to think about something that will get my cock hard, because the more this fucking bitch keeps moaning, the softer my cock seems to be getting.

Standing, I make my way toward the door, turning my head to look back at her. "We're done here. Get dressed and leave."

"B..b..but what about my money?" she stutters

"Collect it on your way out, and don't come back either," I spit.

The guest room is opposite my master suite. Crossing the hall, I go back to my room and shut the big oak door behind me with a bang. This is one place where I actually find peace. The brown-tiled floors, hardwood bed, and floor to ceiling patio doors that have a view of the sandy beach, mountains, and the clear sparkling sea are what help relax me.

This shit has to stop. For ten years I've fucked around, got shitfaced, and worked running these containers, but not once have I ever tried to find out the truth. I've buried my head in a bag of coke and fucked women because I can.

Stripping out of my slacks, I toss them into the laundry hamper and head toward the bathroom. Stepping into the shower, I turn the water on full, blasting myself with a cold burst of water before the heat takes over my body. Resting my head on the white tiles, I let the water run down my back while I think of ways to get the answers I need, because today *has* to be a new day. No more coke, no more fucking around.

Stepping out the shower and looking at my reflection in the mirror, I see the look of determination I had all those years ago, and this time I'm not going to let anything distract me from what I need to know.

The phone rings on the dresser. It's Marco's ringtone, so I place the towel around my hips and head toward it, relishing the feel of the breeze that blows through the open patio doors while breathing in the smell from the fresh sea air. Yes… today will be a new day.

"Yes," I answer.

"Si..Reed, there's been some issues down on the fishing boats, the word is that they think someone escaped from one of your containers," he rushes out.

"What? That's impossible; you know what we have on the containers, and people is not one of those things!" I shout.

He sighs. "I know, I know, but word's getting out. I heard it while I was at the market."

"Okay, I'll speak to the mayor. Can you contact him and get him here for lunch or dinner so we can squash this shit!" I order.

"Of course," Marco replies.

"And Marco…thank you," I say before hanging up. He's been with me through everything and put up with all my shit. The least I can do is be polite.

When I get to the closet, I pick out my cream linen trousers and a white dress shirt. A box catches my eye, so I reach up and pull it down. If I want to make a fresh start then I need to remove temptation, starting with this. The patter of my feet across the tiled floor thuds in my ears. The high has long worn off. This is a massive step, and being faced with this is daunting. Maybe I'm being extreme and need to think about this a little longer. It seems that my brain isn't in control of my body as I enter the large bathroom, only stopping at the double sinks to turn the taps on, and do the same when I reach the jacuzzi bath that sits with a view of the sea. The sound of the water running gives me pause for thought. This is it, now's the time.

I rip the bags individually and pour each one down the drains one by one, looking around as I watch the powder disappear. Finally I rip the last bag, empty the contents and stand. I look down the toilet, and with a flush--that's it. All I have here is gone. Turning around, I switch the taps off and leave the bathroom, jogging down the concrete spiral staircase. My feet thud as I go, the rail squeaking under the pressure of my weight as I go in search of Marco.

Priority number one is to clear this shit up with some random homeless person running around the fishing boats, leading people to believe we have something to do with it. Then time to start uncovering secrets that have been buried.

CHAPTER 2
Maghan

I 'm sitting with my back against the container wall, and it's so cold my whole body is shivering. The journey to wherever I'm headed has been bumpy, kinda like my life, well ever since I was thirteen. Everything I knew just disappeared, and my whole world went downhill. One day I was sitting in my bedroom, listening to my music, and the next Carlos came in and told me I had to leave.

I pull my arms tighter around myself when I remember how I felt when he told me about my brother, Reed. This time it's not the cold air that makes me shiver. I knew the life we were in was dangerous, but I wasn't prepared to lose him, not when he was all I had. I've carried this sick feeling ever since that day. Just learning I was adopted was upsetting, but I hadn't had time to speak to Reed about this. My parents--or "parents"--didn't seem like the kind that would adopt; they didn't seem dedicated to the ones they had. My father was second in command to the Don of the Russo mafia, Carlos's father, which is how we ended up moving into their home when my father was shot in a deal gone

S. E. Robin

sideways. Well, that's what I was told, but who the fuck knows what's real anymore. My mother decided that drugs and alcohol were her comfort, but they ended up being her demise when she overdosed one night after a week-long binge.

My thoughts stop as the container jolts. A scream escapes me before I can stop it, and I quickly raise my hand to cover my mouth, hoping it wasn't loud enough for anyone to hear. I've been in here for weeks, it has to be. I assumed that they would be going across states, not across the fucking ocean. I didn't bring that much food or water with me. I am so hungry, the thought of food makes my tummy rumble. I'm a hot fucking mess.

Wherever I'm headed has to be better than where I've been. Carlos screwed me over big time when he made me leave. I assumed he was sending me to a boarding school, or maybe he'd found my family and wanted me out of the way so he didn't have to take care of me now that Reed was gone. How wrong I was.

I feel a tear hit my bare leg. I didn't realize I was crying; just the thought of what I'd escaped from is upsetting. Thinking back to when he dropped me outside a cold mansion, the driveway overgrown, the paint on the big brown door all scratched and peeling away, the six windows along the top floor all boarded up with ivy growing over the top. It was horrible.

I remember knocking on the door, holding my backpack close to me when *he* came into view. The door squeaked open. Flickering light from the candles barely lit up the entrance, but it was enough. He was a tall man, well built, with dark and threatening eyes, a scarred face, and from what I could see so were both his hands. I was frightened, and from the moment I crossed the threshold that day, my life was forever changed.

We rarely spoke until my sixteenth birthday. That's the day he walked into my dark, dilapidated room. His voice was hoarse, but I knew already what he wanted. I was his gift that he'd been waiting so patiently to "open"; those brief times he did speak to me was always to remind me that I was going to be his. I'm angry at myself for that night. I just froze until it was almost too late, but I was able to prevent him from claiming his gift. I huff out a laugh at the thought of those gaudy candle sticks he had all around the place, and thank fuck I was able to reach one in time to catch him around the head.

I get a tightness in my chest as the memory of his heavy body falling on top of me, but the relief I felt when I pushed him off and sprang to my feet to make a run for the door . . . that feeling of freedom was a high I'd never felt before but one I long to feel again. My actions that night meant that from that day on, I would spend the rest of my days running and constantly looking over my shoulder.

Carlos... he always catches up with you. The past seven years he's sent me to various different men and families. At first it was just for cleaning; he said I needed to pay back what I owed not only for living in his home, but for the candle stick incident too.

It wasn't long until I was being used for more. Carlos had control of me and was using me for his own gain, but he took his eye off the ball, and I had to take the opportunity. I know this container is his and is full of drugs, but it was the quickest and easiest way to get out without being seen. Only now I am god knows where with literally nothing.

A blaring horn sounds and I can hear voices, but they're not talking in a language I can understand. The banging and clattering of chains hitting the container make my head throb, and in moments the whole thing is being hoisted up, and it slowly spins. My tummy churns with the sensation.

The doors are opened with a squeak, and I can hear the men. They all swear and some gag. I'm not surprised. I've been in here for about two weeks--maybe more, maybe less. I kinda lost count, but what I do know is that I had to go to the bathroom somewhere. It's not easy trying to adjust to the bright sunlight as I sneak by the boxes, to get ready to move from the container and out in to the open without being seen.

I watch the men as they move away. One's on the phone, speaking in what could be Spanish or maybe Italian. He is distracted, but the other is pacing up and down next to the container. When his back is turned, I kick one of the boxes into the sea, and the guy on the phone yells for the other guys to come grab the box before it sinks.

When their backs are turned, I make a run for it. I don't get far, but I make it to the end of the marina. Crouching, I secure my hide-out in a small fishing boat. I can smell the food from the restaurants from here, but I need to be careful. I can't let them see me; once that container is gone, I can move from here, then figure out what the fuck I'm going to do.

Night falls after what feels like days. I've watched men loading up another boat with the boxes I shared my journey here with. The ocean is a sparkling blue-green; it's the most beautiful thing I have ever seen. The boat gently rocks back and forth as I watch them work; the sun beams down leaving my skin warm. I feel relaxed, more than I should in my situation, but I'll take anything now, all the small wins. My denim jeans are dirty and ripped, and my t-shirt smells like someone has died in it. I know it was white when I put it on, but now I'm not so sure.

Eventually all the men leave. Some take off on the boat I arrived on, and others with the one just filled. That one is smaller. It's quaint and looks like a fishing boat with its blue stripes and wait, yes, it has a flag flying from the top... I must be in Italy. The nets that attach to the sides must make that a fishing boat; not that I actually know the difference, but I do know I wouldn't want to travel the distance I did on the thing.

Sitting up, I gingerly step out of the boat, making my way past the wealth of yachts and other smaller boats moored in the marina. Someone shouts "*fermare il ladro*". I look around and everyone from the shop fronts are staring at me. My head swivels to see who they're talking to, it can't be me! "Stop the thief," I hear someone else shout.

I start to walk forward, and more people shout *"fermare"*. *Thief*! My heart beats wildly in my chest, my mouth dries, and I do the only thing I can think of.

Run.

CHAPTER 3
Reed

H eading down to the marina, the sun is hot on my skin as I make my way through the cobbled streets I've become so familiar with. The trees that poke out from the mountain walls blow slightly with the occasional breeze I'm thankful for.

Thoughts swirl in my head. Why would people assume that this girl is from our container? I barely oversee the process but we have men, trusted men, that transfer the consignments from the cargo to the fishing boats to go to their final destination. Each boat has a man travel with it to ensure a safe delivery; yesterday, however, we only had one.

The Russos would never deal in trafficking. That's something I would know about, wouldn't I?

I've been out of it for so long now, I probably have no idea what's been going on under my nose. Anger builds inside as I see the shops, restaurants, and cafes come in to view. Taking a deep breath, I take my usual spot at Morellos.

Anna comes rushing out with an espresso, already knowing

what I would order. This is one of the reasons this is my favorite café down here on the front. The service is outstanding, the view is incredible, but most of all Anna knows everything that's going on in the area.

Relaxing back in the cast iron chair, I lift the cup to my lips as Anna watches on, her boney fingers clasped together at the front of her floral apron. "Excellent, as always, Anna," I praise. She's an elderly lady who always makes an effort; her hair is pulled tight in a bun, thin lips painted a plum color with a hint of blush to her cheeks, and her blue eyes sparkle with the compliment.

"So, Anna, what's new?" I ask with a raised eyebrow.

"A girl, scruffy and all dirty on fishing boats." She shudders. Her English is not great, but it's much better than my Italian. "They say she's a thief, they try and stop her but she ran before they get her, now poof." Her hand waves in the air. "She disappear, they think she's from your boat, Mr. Reed." Her bony finger points at me. "Her voice, it's same as you."

My head leans back as I bark out a laugh. Meeting her shocked gaze, I widen my smile. "We don't have people on our containers, Anna, you know that. I only have supplies to ship further up the coast, and also your requests." Smirking at her, I wink and rise to my feet. "Make sure to spread the word for me. I don't want any trouble, and I don't know what I would do if we were unable to bring in your supplies anymore. Where would I get my caffeine fix from then?"

Her hand rises as she waves the towel in my direction, shooing me away. "Sì, Sì," she says as she walks back inside her quaint little coffee shop.

Walking back to the villa, I can't deny I am interested. "*My voice.*" So we have an American running around the marina. My phone rings, pulling me away from my thoughts, and I see Marco's name flash across the screen.

"Hello," I answer.

"Err, Si, Reed, we have a small problem at the villa," he rushes out.

I exhale loudly; this is all I fucking need. "What is it, Marco?"

"Well, it appears your lady friend is here earlier than planned. She was a little out of sorts, shall we say, but I sent her to get freshened up and told her to wait in the guest room." His voice is quieter now.

"What the fuck! You should have sent her packing, Marco, she's not due until this evening," I shout.

"She was soaked head to toe from falling into the ocean. Accidents happen all the time. I couldn't send her away in that state, but there's something different about her. She's not like the others." His tone softens as if he's thinking of her.

"Fucking hell, Marco. I'll be back soon." Huffing, I end the call, and my eyes search the sky as if it's going to give me the answers I'm looking for. It would be a start if I knew what the right fucking questions were to begin with.

Stomping back to the villa, feeling like a petulant child, I see Marco waiting for me as I reach the big iron gates. The flowers line the driveway, with trees neatly trimmed around the edges. The villa is large and imposing to some, but for me this has become home, my sanctuary.

The water trickles as I pass the circular water feature that takes the place of pride in the center of the driveway; concrete fish in the air with water pouring from their mouths. It's an odd choice but it was here when I arrived, and fuck if I'm going to fuck around with shit like that.

"Is she still in the guest room?" I ask as I walk past Marco.

"Yes. Will you be needing anything?" he questions as he turns and follows me as I walk toward the staircase.

Abruptly I stop, feeling Marco bump into the back of me. I raise my brow at him.

"Before you apologize, don't. That was my fault, but I do

have a favor to ask you." Smirking, I pull my bottom lip between my teeth.

"Ooookay." Marco looks at me with uncertainty.

"Please take an eye mask to the guest room and request her to cover her eyes." Smiling to myself, I continue to take the stairs and head to my room, waiting for Marco to inform me she is ready.

A few moments later a knock comes. Marco's face is flushed. "Is she ready?" I question.

Clearing his throat, he starts to shuffle back and forth on his feet. "She said, and I quote, you can go fuck yourself, you sleazy motherfucker." His eyes dart all over the room.

"Mmm, so that's a firm no then." I laugh. "I can see this one's going to be feisty."

Slapping Marco on his shoulder as I walk out of the room, I place my hand on the handle of the guest room door, inhaling as my cock twitches with excitement of what's to come. The women they usually send mostly do as I ask without question. Normally that's what I would prefer, but today that's not what I want.

Bursting through the door, I stand in the shadows as I see her jump at my unexpected entrance. I take a seat in the chair by the open patio doors and watch as she takes slow steps toward the opposite corner, leaning into the wall where I can barely see her face. Her long brown hair cascades down her back, her body is mainly covered by a black t-shirt--*mine if I'm not mistaken*--and long slender legs cross over as she pulls the shirt lower to try to cover herself.

"What's your name?" I ask.

"Hope, and I'm not going to fuck you," she spits out confidently.

My laugh catches us both off guard. Her body pulls back almost like she is offended. "Oh, sugar, you *will* be fucking me. That's why you're here. You came to me, *not* the other way around. Remember that."

21

"No, that's not why I am here!" she shouts. "I came here for a cleaning job. I haven't been in Maiori very long." Her tone lowers but she's still angry; her voice still has that delicious tremor to it. One that my cock seems to enjoy.

"Well, we don't have any vacancies for cleaners. The only position available is for a *personal assistant*, and that entails looking after my needs, and *only* my needs as and when I want them, however I want them. If that isn't of interest then you need to leave." I stand and head toward the door.

"Wait." She clears her throat. "Is that a live in position?" She sounds defeated. I should feel like an asshole but I don't. Women should be the last thing on my mind but she has me intrigued, and as for having her live in... bad idea, but something in my gut is telling me this is the best idea I've had--*or is that my cock telling me that?*

"Yes, it's live in," I hear myself say before I can give anymore thought to it.

"Fine... I'll take it." A huge sigh leaves her as she sinks to the floor and crosses her arms in front of her.

"Perfect. I want you ready tonight after dinner. Wear the mask and sit on the edge of the bed in just the lingerie I will send up for you."

"Fine." Her voice sounds annoyed that she is in this position, but she won't regret it. I will show her what she's been missing. She'll be begging me to fuck her before the night is over.

Returning to my room, I hold on to the warm rails of my balcony, staring at the view and for the first time in a long time, I really smile. There's something about this girl that has me excited, and I can't wait to find out what it is. There was a familiarity that I felt as soon as she opened that beautiful mouth of hers, maybe the familiarity of hearing her accent took me back to a place I haven't been for so long. I can't put my finger on it, but I think I can safely say that I have located the "thief" they've all been talking about since we don't get too many Americans around here.

CHAPTER 4
Meghan

24 hours Earlier

I feel like I've been running for ages. My legs ache like a bitch. I find an alleyway and crouch behind bins, hoping that everyone will forget what they just witnessed.

I hear a voice that comes from the bottom of the alley so I curl up further behind the bins, praying I'm not spotted. I shouldn't have worried; the man is occupied. He throws the trash next to the bin and the aroma smacks me in the face. My mouth waters, and my tummy growls so loud. I squeeze it tightly, looking up and chewing on my bottom lip, hoping he didn't hear.

The man continues chatting on his phone, paying no attention to anything around him, strolling back at a snail's pace toward the door he came from. I'm urging him silently to hurry up; I need to know what's inside these bags.

With a bang, the door closes and plunges the ally into darkness, leaving only the moon as light. The sun from earlier has disappeared and is replaced with a cool breeze, leaving me cold once again.

Diving into the bag, there's boxes of half-eaten pizzas, and like an animal I shovel piece after piece into my mouth, dropping bits on my shirt as I go. If anyone found me like this, they'd think I was possessed. Shaking my head at myself, I know that tomorrow is a new day and I won't have to do this again. I can find something better than this. I know I can.

Sitting on the edge of the marina when everyone has gone feels kinda strange, but this is such a beautiful place. I can't help but think maybe Reed brought me here, that he's watching over me and has helped bring me some place beautiful, some place better. I stand and walk around, looking at what's here: cafes, restaurants, and boutique shops. That's when I spot the notice board, the advert for a live in cleaner. Ripping it from the board, I shove it in my back pocket for later.

I have to do something with my appearance; I stand out like a sore thumb like this. Deciding to walk up and down the marina, I peer into the boats. There has to be something laying around; people would take a spare set of clothes with them all the time, wouldn't they?

Fuck yeah! Looking down into one of the boats, I see some fabric. Reaching down, I grab it and instantly deflate. It's a single light blue shirt, but it's all I have, and right now I can't choose to be picky. I head down to the beach and find the public toilets. Walking down the concrete steps, I peer inside to make sure I'm alone. The toilets are a little grimy but there's soap next to the sink, which means I can have a basic wash down for now.

Looking at myself in the mirror, it's not as bad as I would have thought. I have my hair in a messy bun sitting on top of my head, trying to hide the weeks of grease I have building, and my new shirt hangs just above my knees with the belt from my jeans around my waist. Bending, being careful not to show what I don't have on beneath, I tie the laces on the Converse that I love so much. It makes me sad looking at them now; they look like no one cares for them at all. I'll wash them as soon as I can. After all, give a girl the right shoes, and she can conquer the world, right... according to Marilyn Monroe, and who can argue with her?

Reaching the top of the steps, I can see the night sky turn to dawn. Some people are moving about through the boats, the water rippling as the engines roar to life and they move away from the marina.

Going back to the boat from yesterday, I lie down and close my eyes for a moment.

"Scendi dalla mia barca!!!" a male voice booms, which I guess means *get off my boat.*

"I'm sorry, please don't shout, I'm leaving." Raising my hands in surrender, I step off of the boat, trying to cover myself as I step onto the marina.

The older man is mumbling and waving his hand at me as I walk away. I doubt that he is saying anything good.

There are market stalls lining the streets. I can't believe I slept through them putting these up. I wander through them, taking samples of the bread and fruits as I go, when I hear a man speaking in English.

"Whoever she is. she wouldn't have come off of Mr. Reed's container. He doesn't deal in such things." His voice stern and confident.

People are around him, some speaking in Italian and others in English, all firing questions at him. He just lifts his bags and turns on his heels and walks away, only to look around and state sternly, "Mr. Reed will put this matter to rest, I can assure you, but you should all remember what he does for you before you make such accusations."

Hearing my brother's name brings up emotions I don't want right now. I only wish that it's him that they were talking about, only it's not, and I can't keep wishing for the good things of my past to reappear.

Finding shade next to a coffee shop, I pull the paper out from under my belt. Flattening it out on my palm, I can still see the address; now I just need to find a way to get there.

Following the strong smell of coffee, I make my way into the little coffee shop. The walls are a deep red, and it's filled with brown furniture and the biggest chrome coffee machine I've ever seen fills the counter. A lady comes rushing from behind the counter and ushers me to a seat.

"You like coffee, yes?" she asks with the biggest smile, her hands clasped together at her front.

"Erm, no." I start to shuffle in my seat. "I..I lost my purse, I just wanted directions." I smile back at her.

Her hand flattens to her chests and she gasps. "Oh, that's no good. You have coffee, no charge. Where you want to go?"

"That's so sweet of you, thank you. I'd love a long black." I wouldn't normally accept, but I am not in the position to turn away free food or drink right now. I show her the address on the paper, and her face lights up.

"I'll be back." She rushes off behind the counter.

The kind lady places a cornetto with chocolate spread and a long black in front of me, and my mouth waters just looking at it.

She places her hand on my shoulder. "Enjoy. When finished, I will show you where you need to go."

I watch people come and go until I've enjoyed the first relaxing breakfast I've had in many years. If only life could be like this. This place is paradise, it truly is. If I can land that job then I could do this more often. Chuckling to myself, I feel her hand tap my shoulder.

"You okay? You want me to show now?" Her eyebrows are raised at me; she probably thinks I'm crazy, sitting here laughing to myself.

"Yes, thank you." I rise from the chair and follow her outside. The directions are iffy, but they're better than what I had before. I say goodbye and start in the direction I was given. The cobbled streets and mountain backdrops are something I could definitely get used to, even if I have to walk up this hill every day; the views themselves are worth it.

Getting lost looking at the view, I lose my footing and try to grab something, anything, but there's nothing to hold on to until I feel the cool water hit my skin. Fuck!

Spluttering, I scramble from the water and hold on to the wall, my arm caught in the rope holding the boat tightly to the wall. Finally I manage to pull myself out, but I look like shit *again*!

Straightening my shirt out, wringing the water from my hair and putting it back to a messy bun, I continue to my destination. The sun will dry my clothes… *I hope.*

Approaching the villa, the gravel drive has pretty flowers lining the sides with beautiful bushes around the edges. The fountain in the middle is odd, but if you close your eyes it sounds idyllic. My heart is pounding as I get to the steps. I reach and knock before I can stop myself. The last time I knocked on a door like this, nothing good came from it. This time will be different. This is a fresh start for me, I can feel it.

Footsteps approach from the opposite side of the door, and I can hear the bolts open with a loud clatter. The door glides open to show an elderly man in a suit. He looks friendly.

"Hi," I say, but he ushers me in without so much of a word. I hear the door close behind me. My heart beat picks up and I start to panic.

"Follow me. You can use the guest room to shower, and there are some clothes in the drawers to change into. They might not fit but at least you'll be dry." He clears his throat. "You're here earlier than expected, but Mr. Reed will be back soon. I will let you know when he arrives," he states, then walks away. He hasn't looked at me once after letting me in. I recognize him but can't be sure where from.

CHAPTER 5
Maghan

I wander around the luxurious guest room, running my hand over the linen sheets as I walk over to the patio doors to the warm breeze that welcomes me. The small table and chairs setting there bring a smile to my face; I can see myself having my morning coffee here, or maybe a glass of wine after work. *Getting a little bit ahead of yourself, Maghan.* I chuckle to myself.

Sighing, I realize that I should be getting ready and not relaxing out here. This is not a vacation, even if the place feels and looks like a five-star holiday retreat.

There isn't a huge selection of clothes to choose from, and they're all men's too. Grabbing a black t-shirt before going to the bathroom, I gasp and stop suddenly at the entrance.

This has to be the fanciest bathroom I have ever seen, all white and chrome. I'm not sure I want to touch anything; my fingerprints will spoil it. The shower is huge and could easily fit six people for sure! It even has a seat which I haven't seen of the mountains has to be the best part. I definitely don't have time to use that now, but hopefully I will.

Realizing I've been standing around for ages, I quickly undress and shower. There's shampoo and shower gel that smells divine, all citrusy like fresh oranges. I hear a knock at the door which makes me jump, so I quickly grab a towel and peer my head around the door to see the man from earlier.

"Excuse me. Mr. Reed has returned and has requested you wear this face mask, he would like you to put this on before he comes in."

My mouth drops open. I must look like a fish. I mean, what the actual fuck? What kind of interview is this? "I'm sorry, but you can tell him to go fuck himself, the sleazy motherfucker!"

"Very well, miss, I will let him know. He will be here shortly," he says as he turns and walks out the door.

Drying myself quickly, I put the t-shirt on and come in to the main room and start to pace, when the door bursts open and makes me jump. *Why the fuck am I so jumpy?*

I don't see the man who enters as he is lurking in the shadows, so I move back to the far corner of the room, trying to distance myself from whatever this is. Suddenly I feel self-conscious as I remember what I'm wearing. I tug at the bottom of the shirt, trying to cover myself.

"What's your name?" he asks, breaking the silence. His voice is smooth. He doesn't sound old; his voice sounds sexy as hell! But that's not important.

"Hope, and I'm not going to fuck you," I tell him, trying to stop any shake in my voice from coming out.

He laughs which catches us both off guard. "Oh, sugar, you will be fucking me. That's why you're here. You came to me, not the other way around. Remember that."

What the fuck? Who does this motherfucker think he is? I don't care how sexy his voice sounds, this is not going to happen. "No, that's not why I am here!" I shout. "I came here for a cleaning job. I haven't been in Maiori very long." My voice lowers. I'm so angry and the shake in my voice shows that; I need to control it.

"Well, we don't have any vacancies for cleaners. The only position available is for a personal assistant, and that entails looking after my needs, and only my needs as and when I want them, however I want them. If that isn't of interest then you need to leave." He stands and heads toward the door.

Fuck! I need this. "Wait." I clear my throat. "Is that a live in position?" I exhale, and it feels like an eternity waiting for his answer.

"Yes, it's live in." He sounds bored.

"Fine... I'll take it," I say as I sigh and sink to the floor, crossing my arms in front of me, trying to make myself as small as I possibly can.

"Perfect. I want you ready tonight after dinner. Wear the mask and sit on the edge of the bed in just the lingerie I will send up for you."

"Fine." I'm annoyed by his request, but even more with how quick I took him up on his offer. This is only temporary, it's not like I haven't done this before. I can do it one more time before I find something else. At least this time Carlos isn't in charge.

He leaves the room without a glance back in my direction, and my head drops to my knees. I stand and throw myself onto the comfiest bed I've ever been on, bury my head into the pillows, and scream.

I must have fallen to sleep because a knock wakes me. The room is dark with the moon providing the only light. My face scrunches as the man walks in without me saying anything and pushing a trolly. That's when the aromas hit me.

"Your dinner. We have lasagna with a side salad." He bends down and pulls a box from the bottom shelf. "Mr. Reed wanted you to have this, he insists that you follow his earlier instructions." He nods his head and leaves.

Pushing myself off of the bed, I look over the food, ignoring the box. Picking up the plate, I start shoveling the food in like I haven't eaten before. Stepping out onto the balcony and taking a seat, I place the plate down and decide to eat properly and savor the food and actually taste what's been given to me. I have a feeling I'm going to need to take all the small things here and enjoy the small perks I get: the great food, the luxury baths, and the peacefulness to just stop and think for a while rather than keep running.

"Miss," the man says, clearing his throat.

"What's your name?" I ask

"Marco." His head bows. "I'm here to clear your plates. You need to get ready. Mr. Reed will be here in thirty minutes, please be ready."

Looking down, I try to smile at him but I can't bring myself to. This is the start, and I only hope I'm ready.

Opening the box, I can't believe what I'm looking at: red lace matching underwear with a black eye mask. Taking everything out, my hand touches something small, hard, and rectangle. Picking it up, I see he's also included lipstick. My eyes roll when I see the color; red for me. This guy is an absolute asshole. I grab the whole box and stomp my way to the bathroom to do as I was asked. I change into what he has for me and it's not quite the right size. The bra is a little small so my tits are spilling over the top slightly, but the thong isn't bad. After applying the lipstick, I look at myself and quickly look away. I don't want to see myself this way, selling myself once again, but this *will* be the last time. I *have* to repeat this to myself. This is *not* who I am.

Perching on the end of the bed, I place the eye mask over my eyes and wait.

I hear the door open and close quietly, and nothing else for what feels like forever. I try to work out where he is but I have no idea, until…

"You look beautiful when you follow orders. Spread your legs, I want to see you." His voice is commanding but it's smooth as fucking silk.

Working my jaw, holding back the fuck you I want to yell in his face, I slowly part my legs.

"Perfect. I see the sizing is a little off; next time that won't happen." His finger runs across the top of my chest.

My breathing picks up, my chest rises and falls quickly, and I can hear my heart beating wildly in my ears.

His voice lowers as he leans toward my ear. "Time to play." His tongue runs across the shell of my ear and ends with sucking my lobe. I feel a sharp bite and flinch back but feel my nipples harden at the sensation.

His hands skim over my shoulders, pulling the cups of my bra down and exposing my tits. His hands continue their journey downward, spreading out when each hand goes to a hip, and squeeze hard. Pulling me so I am closer to him, he runs his hands up and down my thighs.

"Arch your back slightly, keep your face forward," he commands.

Arching my back, my hands slightly behind me, I face forward.

"Exactly like that! Fuck, you have no idea what I want to do to you," he says as he stands, and I hear rustling then the clinking of metal hitting the floor. My chest rises and falls faster, my legs close slightly as I feel the throb between my legs. I need to ease the ache that's building.

He tuts. "I don't think so, sugar, they stay open until I say so."

A whimper leaves my lips. What is this guy doing to me? Why am I reacting to him this way? My body is betraying my mind. I want his touch; my body is craving to have his tongue lick more than just my fucking ear! But my mind and body are at war.

My hands grip the sheets as I feel his nose run up my slick slit. I'm so embarrassed. He'll notice, there's no way he won't. He inhales deeply, and I feel my face burn up.

"You're fucking soaked. I can smell how much you want

this. Tell me." His voice is deeper, huskier, and images run through my mind of what I want him to do as I try to still myself.

"F…fuck you," I stutter.

A moan rips from me as his tongue runs over my panties. *Fuck.* I want so much more than that. His thumb runs mindlessly over my nipple while his nose runs along the inside of my thigh. I lift my hips to the side to get him back where I need him most, and he stands abruptly.

"Oh, sugar, you want something? You know all you have to do is ask." I can hear a smile in his voice, and I know I am fucked. But you know what? Fuck it. If I can get something more than a bed and breakfast from this deal then I'm going to embrace it and enjoy the fucking ride. It's about time I had some fun.

CHAPTER 6
Reed

My cock is throbbing as I look at this beauty perched on the end of the bed. I run my hand up and down my length, squeezing to give me some relief. Her legs are spread with her tits exposed, and I want to fucking devour her. One taste of that delicious cunt wasn't enough. She will give in, and when she does, I'm going to enjoy having her beg me for more.

Smelling her desire, feeling how soaked she is for me, I know she wants me. She just has to give in. The desire in her voice when I hear the "fuck you" from her plump, sexy, ruby-red lips makes me want to fuck it right from her mouth. The thought of seeing red painted on my cock makes precum leak from my tip.

Looking at her face, the pained expression when I tell her to tell me what she wants, I can see she's at war with herself. Her mind is at war with her body, and it's fucking glorious to watch.

"Touch me, I want to feel your tongue on me." Her voice a whisper, almost like she doesn't want to want this.

"Oh, sugar, you've forgotten your manners," I say, a laugh

escaping me. "I'm not here to take orders from you, so what do you say?" My hands are on her legs, getting closer to her wet heat.

"Please. Touch me, please."

"Good girl." The praise leave my lips without a thought. A moan escapes her and her panties dampen. It looks like my little fire cracker likes hearing me praise her more than she'd like to admit. I shake my head at myself. I don't praise women, they're here to do as I ask and then I leave. I don't care if they're satisfied, so what the fuck just happened? Why does her reaction have so much effect on me?

Bending down, I pull at her panties and she automatically lifts so I can remove them. Taking in the sight of her glistening pussy makes my mouth water; watching her squirm is so fucking hot.

Leaning down, my head dips forward and I lick slit to clit, thinking I'll take this slowly. But as I move back, her hand flies to my head to hold me back in place, her hips pushing forward to meet my mouth.

"Please don't stop, please," she begs.

Her hands grip my hair. This woman is so fucking sexy that my resolve breaks. Standing, I lift her and toss her further up the bed. My cock aches watching her perky tits bounce; her dusky pink nipples are pebbled and calling to be sucked.

Getting on the bed, I run my hands over her body, sit her up, and turn her to face the headboard.

"Put your hands on here," I command.

My hands move her hair, pulling it down her back. Then I release her bra, watching her breasts spill free as I toss the fabric to the floor. She is a work of fucking art. She jumps when I run my hands down over her ass, adjusting her legs and opening them wider.

"What are you doing?" Her voice is uncertain.

I move around and position my head between her legs.

"Take a seat, sugar, if you want it take it." I smirk. Instantly she does as she's told, and fuck. Watching her ride my face, taking what she wants, makes me want to please her. She throws back her head and I feel her hair touch my chest. I can feel everything, every sensation, as one hand glides through my hair and pulls.

"Oh god, fuck…" she pants. "I'm so close, fuck."

A growl leaves me, hearing her panting.

"Oh fuuuck, ahhh." She stills on top of me, but my tongue doesn't ease, and I continue working her sensitive bud. Her pussy pulses as I feel her come, taking every last drop. I know this will never be enough.

Her body sags, thinking this is over, but I'm not through with her just yet. Quickly I slide her down my body, and with one hand I position my cock at her entrance. In one thrust, my cock is surrounded by her tight wet heat. *Fuck, she feels fucking good.*

Nails pinch my chest as she hisses at my intrusion, and my cock pulses at the pinch of pain.

Placing my hands behind my head, I look at her sitting on my cock.

"Fuck me, sugar. Let me see you slide up and down my cock, let me feel how wet my cock makes you." I move my hips to urge her on and she begins. She's like a goddess.

Fuck. "Good girl. You like riding my cock, don't you?" I say, my jaw working. Her pussy grips my cock and she groans at the praise.

"You like being my good girl, don't you, sugar?" I ask, bringing my hand up and running it along her leg.

"God yes, fuck, you feel so good," she pants as she bounces up and down on my cock.

"You're making my cock nice and wet. You should see how wet you're making me, I can feel it dripping down my balls." Her head tosses back as I adjust us so we are facing each other. I want to rip the mask off of her face but now's not the time.

I move forward and suck her bottom lip, surprising myself as I've never kissed a woman I've been with. It's too personal, but her lips are too enticing to resist. She opens up and her tongue forces its way in to mine and the kiss becomes urgent, passionate, and we're battling for control.

I pull back as her head comes forward to continue, but my head tells me it's enough. I need to think about this. What am I doing?

My hand runs up her body, stopping at her neck and gripping slightly.

"Yes, fuck yes, please." Her voice is hoarse as she fucks me faster, harder.

My mouth goes to her nipples. I start to suck and nip, my hand gripping her neck tighter each time.

"Please. Suck harder, please," she begs.

So she likes a little bit of pain. Let's see how much…

I bite her nipple and her pussy clenches as moans leave her. The harder I suck, bite, and grip her neck, the closer she gets to coming.

"That's it, oh god, please, just like that, ye… yeah. Oh fuck, I'm gonna come."

"Fuck yeah, that's it. Be a good girl and come for me," I say.

I feel it before I hear her. My cock feels like it's in a vice and I can't hold on anymore. I roar as I fill her up. Fuck, this is the most intense feeling I've ever had with a woman.

She falls onto me and I don't, for the first time, move to get out of there. My cock is still buried deep inside of her.

Bolting backward, I see my cum dripping from her pussy, and fuck me, that's a sight I won't forget. The urge to push it back in is a new one and something I try to push to the back of my mind.

"What's wrong?" I ask.

"We didn't use protection." She looks panicked.

"We don't need to worry about that, you know I normally only use an agency so I am clean, I'm not concerned," I state. "You wouldn't have gone bare if you weren't taking precautions sugar" What she doesn't know is it's the first time I've ever gone bare--and if she thinks it'll be the last, she can think again.

"You have your cleaners checked? What the fuck is this place?" Her head turns in the direction of my voice so quick I'm surprised she doesn't give herself whiplash.

"Cleaners." I laugh. "Sugar, I haven't recruited for cleaners. I told you, the ladies I employ are for my pleasure."

"Hookers," she spits.

"Escorts," I reply.

"Well, I am *not* an escort." She huffs.

"No, sugar, *you're* not, you, well… you're mine," I tell her confidently.

CHAPTER 7
Meghan

I can't believe I played his stupid fucking game. I gave in. *Please touch me.* What the fuck was I thinking? I mean, I clearly wasn't. My pussy was doing the thinking for me! I wanted to have fun but to beg for it... well, that's something else.

Plenty of men have called me a good girl before, but it always grossed me out. Yet with him, I just want to hear it again and again.

Sitting on the balcony, wrapped in a linen bed sheet while watching the sea as it sparkles and gently moves back and forth, I replay the evening in my head. *You're mine.* What does that even mean? He hired me to fuck him; he doesn't own me. I don't belong to anyone, not anymore, and I don't want to either. Or so I keep trying to tell myself.

Determined to forget about how I felt tonight, I go to the bed and sink into the mattress, trying to ignore the scent he left behind. It's masculine sandalwood, citrusy, and something that I can't put my finger on, but it's intoxicating.

Huffing to myself, I toss the covers to the floor and move to the chair in the corner of the room. It looks soft with red velvet cushions and a throw over the black arms. Throwing the cushion across the room, I realize that this chair is as hard as rock, but it'll have to do because I am not sleeping in those sheets until they've been changed.

Tossing and turning, I give up on sleeping, and morning comes eventually. Marco comes in with an extravagant breakfast, and he is shocked when I inform him I won't be requiring anything as I will be out this morning. If this is my life now then I will be having my breakfast and morning coffee in the one place that I've found comfort: Morellos.

One small problem with that plan is not having any money to my name.

"Marco, where is Mr. Reed?" I inquire.

"He's in his office; he has business he has to attend to. You should stay in here until he is finished." He nods his head confidently.

Laughing, I look at Marco. "You're serious. Well, that's not happening. Where is his office? I need to talk to him." I'm shaking my head in disbelief.

"I'm sorry, miss, you cannot go to his office. I will try his line to see if he is available to speak to you, if you insist." Huffing, he reaches into his suit jacket and pulls out his phone.

"Yes, Marco, I do," I reply, rolling my eyes at how ridiculous this is.

Tapping away on his cell, Marco's phone rings and he answers. I hear him tell who I assume is Mr. Reed that I would like to leave this morning and want a word.

"Sugar, how are you this morning," he drawls.

"Fan-fucking-tactic. I want to go out but I want my money for last night," I rush out, my heart beating at how sharp I'm being.

He laughs. "Oh, you now want payment for your services? Last night you weren't a hooker or an escort."

"That's all still true but apparently I'm yours, whatever that means, so unless I am able to get a job, I need money for clothes and food," I spit.

"Firstly, you are *mine*, that means no one else will touch you. Secondly, I'm the one in control here, sugar, so if I say no then you will stay in your room until I decide otherwise." I can hear the smirk on his voice.

"You know what? Fuck you!" I shout.

I toss the phone at Marco, throw the door open, and hear it bang against the wall. My feet pound along the tile floors to the top of the staircase as I look around at Marco when he calls my name, only to slam into a solid wall of muscle.

Fuuuuuuck!

"Who are you? Get the fuck off of me!" I shout, kicking my legs out as the man holds my back to his front. His hand reaches up to cover my mouth.

The guy doesn't answer me, but I know who it is as we start toward my room, his scent engulfing me.

"Marco, get the ties," he instructs.

I am placed on the bed, my arms and legs kicking at him until I see the gun peek through the jacket he has on, and I instantly freeze.

Who the fuck is this guy? My body lies limp on the bed and I allow him to tie my legs and arms to each corner of the bed. The shirt I'm wearing has inched up my thighs to expose my panty-clad pussy, but I'm too shocked to even care about what he can and cannot see.

Shrugging off his jacket, he doesn't seem in the slightest bit concerned that he's carrying, which means he's used to it. His eyes roam over me, and he looks like he wants to devour me. I can see the lust in his translucent blue eyes. It's like looking into the ocean. He has a short beard that I remember the feel of so well between my legs. My pussy clenches at the memory.

I don't get to study him much longer before he pushes my hair from my face and our eyes meet. The blue of his eyes turn stormy as he grips my chin between his thumb and forefinger, pulling my head so we're looking at each other head on.

He pushes my head back and curses.

"Who the fuck are you?" he shouts.

"W..what? You know who I am, my name's Hope," I stutter. I start to fidget as I watch him pace the floor of the bedroom, his hands working back and forth through his thick brown hair.

"Really, and you don't have any other names? Because you look fucking familiar," he spits.

"I don't know what you're talking about, of course not," I say, hoping I sound more confident than I feel.

"Answer me this, Hope, do you have any family? Brothers?" He stalks toward me, his eyes fixed on mine. I have no idea what this is about, but I do the only thing I can do: tell him the truth. I don't want to go through this, but I don't want to die either.

"No, not anymore. They died." I look away from him.

His laugh is dark. "I hope that's true." Leaning over the bed, he rips my shirt open. My nipples pebble when the cold air touches them, and his hand reaches for my neck and grips tight.

"I really, really hope that's fucking true, sugar." He reaches into his holster, grabbing his gun. I gasp for breath as he releases my neck briefly. His hand goes to his back to pull out an attachment, and he looks at me while he screws it onto the end. My mouth goes dry, I feel like I have cotton wool clogging up my throat. I try swallowing but I can't seem to get any moisture. My tongue continues to lick at my lips, but still nothing.

I watch as he walks to the opposite side of the bed and leans forward so he is half on the bed. He raises the gun and I hold my breath, expecting the gun to go off, but it gently touches along my jaw to my chin, then he taps my lips.

"Open up," he commands.

My mouth drops open without hesitation and a whimper escapes. My chest rises and falls with my heart beating wildly.

"Suck." His command comes with his eye brow raised and a smirk on his perfectly kissable lips.

I take the gun in my mouth and suck, but the ability to swallow is gone. The moisture I lacked before all gathers in my mouth and starts to spill down my chin. He pushes further until I feel the tip hit my gag reflex and I start to choke.

"I can see you need to work on that if you're struggling with my Beretta." He winks, *he fucking winks at me.*

He pulls it out with a pop. His eyes roam down as his hand moves my panties to the side.

"It looks like you enjoyed that, sugar," he says as he runs the tip of his Beretta over my sensitive bud. "Do you think it's loaded?" he says, laughing.

He swiftly moves the gun back and shows me that there are bullets loaded inside. Oh my god, he's a crazy son of a bitch! Jumping slightly, I feel the cool metal touch my lips as he teases around my bud.

"What do you want, Hope?" The question comes but he doesn't look at me; his eyes stay fixed on my pussy. I whimper but stay silent. My body is betraying me again. I want to feel him inside me, feel his tongue explore me. Sweat trickles down the side of my head, and I try to even out my breathing and concentrate on that rather than the tingling sensation I have building below.

His hand stills and he looks up. I start to protest, I don't want this to stop, but this is wrong. So fucking wrong.

"You have one more chance, sugar." He taps gently on my pussy with his gun facing sideways. "All you have to do is ask."

"I want to feel you," I whisper.

His brow raises and his head shakes. I know he is going to leave, and before I can even think, "Please, please. I want to feel you," blurts out. He has me exactly where he wants me.

Smirking at me, he comes forward. Taking my neck in a tighter grip, he slides his Barretta inside my pussy. I feel his breath on my cheek as he comes close to my ear. "Do you think you've been a good girl?"

Trying to stop my hips from moving, my head shakes no.

"Good, you would be right. Do you think you deserve me to fuck you, with or without my cock?" he whispers.

"P..please. I'll be good, I promise," I say, begging him.

"Oh, I don't doubt you'll try, but I think you have secrets. I want to know," he says as his hand moves in and out, working his gun back and forth and making me moan at the odd sensation. His grip gets tighter and I struggle to take any breaths. My orgasm is building. I can hear my juices as he moves, but I'm too far gone to be ashamed of the wetness pooling between my thighs.

Just as I am about to come, he removes the gun and releases my neck from his grip.

I look at him, dazed from what's happening right now.

"Bad girls don't deserve to come, sugar." He smirks at me as my head falls back against the pillow.

CHAPTER 8

Reed

That moment I looked into her dark chocolate-brown eyes, my heart skipped a beat. I would have said that I would recognize them anywhere, but it can't be her. I had to ask, but she died ten years ago. Her name's Hope, not Maghan!

She feels different. I feel different when I'm with her. The hole in my chest doesn't feel as big. *Fuck*! I slam my bedroom door shut behind me and swipe the contents off of the dresser. Hearing them smash eases some tension that's been building since I left her room.

My minds been playing tricks on me ever since. What if it's *her*? What if after all these years she's back and she found her way to me? What if Carlos lied and she didn't kill herself? So many what ifs. Pacing, I'm pissed I flushed all the coke; what I would do to get high right now. Normally I would get high and fuck to clear my mind, but my cock's still throbbing from seeing her sprawled across the bed, taking everything I had to give her. Watching, aching for release as I left her there, needy and wanting what only I am able to give her. As much as I wanted to fuck her, something held me back.

I have to be sure… she can't be my sister. *Well, you're not actually related; she was adopted,* I try to assure myself. The thing is, I don't have to do much reassuring. Now that I've had a taste, she's mine and nothing will stop me from having her—not a single thing in the world. She's mine and not a single fucking thing will change that.

My ears start ringing as I kick past the shit all over the floor, on and off the ringing goes and it won't stop. It takes me a while to realize it's not in my head but it's my phone that's going. The light comes on and it comes to life again with the persistent fucking ringing. Carlos's name flashes across the screen when I bend to pick it up, thankful that I didn't crack the screen when it flew across the floor.

Accepting the call, I don't get a chance to speak.

"What the fuck, Reed, why aren't you answering your phone?" he spits. "We have issues here, I may need to come and see you. Be ready when I next call and don't make me wait." The line goes dead before I can answer him.

Typing away, I fire a text because what the fuck was that?

> Hey man, what the fuck was that, what's going on?

Throwing my phone on my bed, I head to the shower. I hoped that phone call with Carlos would have eased the ache in my cock but it hasn't.

Turning the faucet on to the coldest setting, I strip and take my throbbing cock in my hand and squeeze. A groan leaves me. Shaking my head as my eyes close, all I can see is her. Her lips parted, moaning, and her hips moving to take my Beretta deeper. I hiss as the cold water hits my back. Opening my eyes, I move to cover myself from head to toe in the coolness of the water. Nothing, not a fucking thing, is going to dull this ache, so instead I grip my shaft and thrust slowly, my head leaning against the tiles, one hand against the cold surface, and I'm taken back to her. I can hear her moans clearly, the smell of the juiciest oranges envelops me like she's here, it's like they're not in my head at all, and fuck, I wish they weren't.

My movements turn frantic as I feel myself getting closer when I hear a hiss and feel hands slide around my body.

Turning around, I stare into the dark eyes. Lust fills them; she wants me as much as I want her. Before I say anything, she drops to her knees, still looking up at me, and it's sexy as fuck. But if she thinks I'm going to let her have my cock like this then she's fucking wrong. Seeing her on her knees, looking at me like this—fuck, it's taking all of my restraint not to force my cock down her throat and feel how much my little firecracker can take —but not now, not today.

Pulling her hair, I drag her back off of her feet. Her hands flies to her head, a groan leaves her in pain—but as her hard nipples run along my body, a groan leaves her and she starts to wriggle in my grasp.

"Sugar, you insist on being a bad girl," I whisper. Her neck turns and I feel her nails gently run over my pecs and down my arms.

"I didn't say you could leave your room today, why are you here?" I question, my cock aching as she continues to wriggle back and forth.

"Please, I want you. I need to come. I'm sorry." Her voice is husky and wanting, so fucking needy. It's sexy as fuck.

"Get out the shower and go on the balcony. Wait for me there… naked," I tell her.

Her eyes round and her mouth opens and closes like she wants to tell me no, but she wants release more. Watching that battle is turn on.

Seeing her walk away with her pretty little ass swaying as she does brings a smirk to my face. That'll be mine too…soon.

Drying off quickly, I make my way to the balcony and see her sitting in the corner out of view. I know that nobody can see what goes on here, but she doesn't, and that's what will make this fun. The black metal railings have gaps so she will think she's going to be seen from below if anyone walks past. There is no way in this world that I would let another person see her like this! Her body belongs to me, all her pleasure belongs to me, and *she* belongs to me… it's that simple.

"Stand in the middle of the balcony facing out. Spread your legs and bend so I can see your pretty little pussy," I command.

Watching her, I see the indent in her cheeks as she chews the inside, her eyes darting left and right, looking to see if she can see anyone around. Rising from her seat, she swallows loudly as she makes her way to the center of the balcony, her breathing picking up, steps uncertain, but I can smell her arousal.

"You're facing the wrong way, sugar." Tutting at her, she nods her head and slowly turns to face the stunning view, a view that normally relaxes me but nothing can beat the view I have right now as I sit back with my legs spread out, my gray sweat pants tenting, not hiding my desire for the beauty in front of me.

Her forearms rest on top while her legs slowly part, edging her soft ass closer and closer to me, showing me her glistening pussy and her puckered hole all there ready to be taken. Soon!

I start to walk along the balcony, her head moving from side to side following me.

"You've been a bad, bad girl, Hope, and you know what happens to bad girls, don't you?" I ask her, wanting to hear her response.

"N..no," she stutters.

Gripping the back of her neck, I say, "Keep your eyes forward." My hand continues down the arch of her soft back until reaching her ass. She flinches which makes me chuckle. "You had enough, sugar?"

"No, please don't stop," she rushes out.

So eager. I knew she'd want this, that I could get her begging me. I squeeze her ass; my mouth waters for a taste as her moans fill the warm air.

My hand raising, I land a smack on her right cheek and then squeeze to ease the sting. I chuckle as a blush rises on her face. "Bad girls get punished." I follow with five smacks on each cheek, squeezing after each, watching her pretty ass color red. The more I do, the louder she moans, and seeing my mark on her skin has my cock leaking. Shaking my head, I can see that my firecracker is enjoying this more than I thought she would.

Oh, she has no idea how much I want to fuck her, but I'm supposed to be waiting until I find out more about her. The fact that she's testing me is making me want to make her pay even more.

"How much do you want my cock, sugar?" My voice is close to breaking. Her head turns quickly to look at me; her hair is stuck to her face where the heat and arousal have made her sweat.

"Badly, please, I need your cock, I want to feel you inside me." Her pleading voice is raspy.

"Come warm my cock, sugar." There's a smile in my voice, and I see her raise her eyebrow at my command. Leaning forward, I reach for her as she makes her way over.

Releasing myself, I move so she can straddle me as I rest my back on the cushions in the chair. Her tits pressing against my chest makes a groan leave us both.

Pulling her up, I move my hand and guide my cock to her entrance, running the tip back and forth between the slippery slit.

"You feel fucking good, sugar," I tell her as I push into her tight wet heat and hold her hips still when she goes to rise.

"That's not what's happening here. You needed my cock and wanted to feel me inside you," I say, looking at her mouth drop open. "And I, well, I want you sitting close to me, sugar, not knowing where I end and you begin, and this is fucking perfect." My lips crash into hers and I nip, suck, and bite as we kiss like we're starving, both fighting to take control. My tongue reaches hers and I swallow her moans, feeling her pussy grip my cock like it's a fucking vice.

I can feel her everywhere. Her hands roam all over my body, exploring me like I'm a map of the world. My heart's beating, my cock throbs feeling her take what she wants, from what little I'm allowing.

My mouth moves away from her bruised lips and finds her dusky pink nipples, pebbled and inviting me to take them. My mouth takes turns sucking and nipping. I grip harder on her hips, stopping the movements she continues to attempt to make, and her pleas become closer and closer. I know she's almost there; her breathing has picked up, her moans are louder.

"Ah, fuck yes, that's it, please keep doing that, suck harder," she begs. "Fuck, ye.. yes, I'm going to…" she pants and begs.

I lift her off of my cock. Her face is dazed but her hand goes between her legs to finish what's been started. I don't thinks so, any pleasure she has comes from me and me only, unless I say so.

I reach for her hands and pull her to the bed in the room, going out and across to the guest room and tossing her to the middle of the bed. Reaching for the straps, I tie her back to the bed.

"Remember what I said, sugar, bad girls don't get to come." I wink at her as I make my way out of the door, hearing her shout fuck you as I leave.

Laughing, I head back to the room and do the only thing I can: head to the shower and find the release I need so fucking badly.

CHAPTER 9
Maghan

Struggling against the restraints, I start to scream a curse at the man who I both hate and want at the same time.

Starting right now, he can go fuck himself. He continues to get me to the edge and leave me hanging. What a jerk! Who does that?

Rubbing my legs together to ease the ache he's left me with, I try to get myself off but huff at the pitiful attempt.

Screaming to the top of my lungs, I shout at him over and over but get no response. My voice is hoarse, my body aches from the position I'm lying in, and it isn't long until I start to drift off to sleep.

When I wake I feel a soft morning breeze blowing through the doors, the smell of coffee awakens my senses, but I feel odd. I must have slept for hours. My tummy rumbles loudly as I think about missing all meals yesterday, but I glance up and see the tray glistening on the trolly at the foot of my bed.

My arms are no longer tied to the posts and I have a sheet covering me. Someone must have come in. My cheeks heat at the thought that Marco might have discovered me like that.

I recognize the red and white logo on the coffee cup as Morellos, urging me to move from the bed quicker than normal, my legs stumbling slightly as I stand.

The pastries look delicious and I grab one while I take a long sip of the nectar which is the long black, so smooth it practically glides down my throat.

Looking back, I notice a note with my name across the front.

> Hope
> Good Morning Sugar,
>   I have business to attend to. Don't worry, I haven't forgotten about you. I will be able to see and play with you while I am gone.
>   In the meantime, stay put and do as I ask.
>   Oh, and remember only good girls get rewarded.
>   R x

What the actual fuck! See me? Looking around, I rush over to the door and push down on the handle and a shock curses through me. I inhale at the harshness of the current, and my hand goes to my neck as I jump back. Tears build in my eyes as I run to the bathroom, look in the mirror, and see what's around my neck.

Warm tears run down my cheeks as my chest heaves in heavy sobs. I brush my hand gently across the most beautiful silver choker with diamonds embedded into the center. How can something so beautiful cause pain?

My legs give out. I sink to the floor and huddle up in the fetal position and just cry until I have no tears left.

Days go by, and the only person I see is Marco when he brings me food and new books to read. I haven't seen or heard anything from Mr. Reed since he left me hanging or since that shitty shock.

Marco brings my supper and informs me that Mr. Reed is on the phone for me. Well, fuck that and fuck him.

"Sugar, how are you?" he practically purrs down the phone, and just hearing his voice brings my pussy alive.

I don't answer. I need to stay silent. He collared and shocked me!

"Ah, so you're not speaking to me. We will soon see about that. I have some instructions in the envelope and you will follow them. You know how I know that?" he questions. "Because I know deep down you *want* to be a good girl, you *want* to please me." His tone lowers, and he doesn't allow for a response—even if I wanted to—as he hangs up.

God, this man is frustrating. What I worry about is I don't think he's wrong.

Handing the phone back to Marco, he hands me a box and leaves. The lock echos throughout room as he turns it to secure me inside.

Tossing the box on the bed, the contents fall out and my mouth gapes at what's inside. The silky red nightdress feels amazing, and when I reach to see what's underneath...my eyes widen at the variety of dildos and the sizes. Some I can see will never fit, that I am sure of! What am I supposed to do with these?

Pulling at the note which is stuck under the lid, I read what he wrote:

Sugar,
Practice makes perfect and I want to see you making use of your time alone. I want you to be able to swallow my cock whole, like all good girls can.
   R x
PS. I will be watching...

Scrunching up the note, I throw it across the room. This man makes me so angry but hearing him has me tied up in knots. I want what I shouldn't want. I want to please him but I know I shouldn't want that… I am so confused right now.

Picking up the toys, I move to the bed and feel the plastic shaped cock between my small hands. My eyes close, and I think of his voice as my hands find their way down my body. Removing my t-shirt, I lie naked on the bed.

My legs drop wide as I lick the tip before sucking it into my mouth, wetting as much as I can. Making a loud popping noise as I remove it from my lips, I rub it over one pebbled nipple as my other hand teases and pinches the other.

Placing the dildo at my entrance, I tease it back and forth, swirling around my sensitive bud before I thrust it inside in one motion. My wrist starts to move in time with my hips when I get a shock that makes me drop the dildo and fall to my side.

I hear a chuckle all around the room. I can't see anyone, but I would recognize it anywhere.

"You are not following instructions very well, sugar." His voice is full of amusement.

"Where are you? Why the fuck have you got this attached to me?" I yell at him.

"I told you I'd be watching you, and I am. The room has been fitted with cameras, I can see *everything* you do." His laugh sounds demonic. "Someone is being a *very* bad girl." This time he sounds serious.

I pull myself up so I am against the headboard, and grab the sheet to cover me. "Why are you doing this to me? I thought you wanted someone to have sex with."

"Do you think you've earned that yet, sugar? Ever since I gave you what you wanted… *my* cock deep inside your wet heat, you haven't done anything I've asked." His tone is bored as he huffs. "Look, this is frustrating for us both, but you have the rules. All you have to do is abide by them, then we will both get what we want."

"H..how long are you going to keep me here?" My voice stutters, betraying me.

"I will be back when you least expect it, and I want you to be ready for me when I am," he commands.

"What if I don't want to?" I spit back at him, crossing my arms across my chest defiantly.

"Oh, sugar, we both know you do," he purrs.

CHAPTER 10

Reed

I've been watching her for days, but speaking with her tonight has me on edge. I've reached out to my contacts to find out what they can on my little fire cracker.

I stand facing the mountains, inhaling the fresh air, my head clear for what feels like forever. This morning has to be the first I haven't woken with a muzzy head, one that comes from alcohol and coke. It's refreshing, only now I'm struggling with the temptation that's the beauty in the room across the hallway.

Laughing to myself at the thought of her getting more and more agitated as the days pass but seeing her slowly break strangely gives me inner peace, especially when I know that I'll be the one that will put her together again piece by piece. By the time I've finished with her, she'll be begging for me.

I feel the vibration of my cell phone and see Sawyer's name flash across the screen. What he can't find isn't worth finding.

"Sawyer, what did you find?" I ask bluntly.

"Hello to you too, boss." He chuckles. "Look, I have got a lot. It's fucked up, so I hope you're sitting down."

I make my way to the balcony and sit. Looking out to the

mountains, my mind wanders to the time I had Hope out here, and my cock twitches instantly. *Now's not the fucking time - concentrate!*

"Shoot, I'm all ears." My jaw clenches, waiting for what's to come.

"I'll email the files over, but first things first. Maghan... I don't know how to tell you this, man, but she didn't die. The info I got was that the body they used was a Jane Doe they found on the streets." He releases a heavy sigh. "Look, I don't have all the details yet, man, but what happened to her over the past ten years... Well, you can probably guess. Carlos has been hiding a lot of shit, and to be honest, I think I'm only just scratching the surface."

I interrupt him. "What are you saying? Carlos was selling Maghan to the highest bidder?" I can feel the anger rising as I clench my fists.

"Basically that's exactly what he was doing. From the information I have, she was under the impression you'd been killed. He made up some kind of story, but I don't have all of those details." I can hear him rummage paper as he speaks.

"Where's Maghan now? I need to find her, let her know she's safe." I can hear the desperation in my voice but I don't care. I want to see her, I need to make sure she's away from Carlos.

"Err, well, I was getting to that, and this is the bit where you probably want a seat." He starts to chuckle. "You asked me to look into Hope, find out what I could, and all roads lead back to Maghan."

"What? So I was right, she's my fucking sister?" I shout.

"Euh euh euh, nope! She is not your sister. I mean, not really. Turns out the papers you had are accurate, she was adopted—but to your dad not your mom," he says smugly.

"What the fuck does that mean? We had the same parents." My hand runs back and forth through my hair, pulling at the ends.

"Maghan Carter, AKA Hope now, was adopted, but the

person who adopted her was Carlos Senior's right hand man--your father--because no one actually knows who her real father is. But, and this is a big fucking but, and Carlos Junior's biggest issue... is you," he says gravely.

"Me? What the fuck, what am I missing here?" I spit.

"You're older than Carlos. Not only older, but also Carlos Senior's first born."

I can't hear anything else, I don't have a clue what he is fucking talking about.

"First born? What the actual fuck are you talking about?" My voice is a whisper.

"It appears Carlos Senior had, shall we say, a moment which led to you and the rest is history until he made sure you came into the family business. He was happy that you were being brought up with his underboss, but Carlos Junior found out who you were, and after that things went south," he mutters.

"The car accident," I say, "as I thought, wasn't an accident, was it?"

"I haven't got that far, but the will I found—which is the only one on record—names you as sole beneficiary aside from Caitlin receiving a mention. I would suggest that's a safe bet."

"Fuck! Does Caitlin know?" I smile, thinking of her. I haven't spoken to her in so long. "Wait, tell me she's safe, that he hasn't hurt her too!"

"She knows. I've made contact. She's living with Jax, head of the Riveria Mafia." Another sigh leaves him. "I'm telling you, that's a story for another day, but she's been trying to contact you for years. She found out that you were the beneficiary but couldn't trace you."

"I'm just grateful she's safe, I'm grateful they both are." I sit down heavily on the patio chair, making it push back and squeak along the tiles. My body winces at the sound. "I appreciate this more than you know, Sawyer. When you have more, let me know."

"You got it. Keep your eye on Carlos and the containers; something feels off."

"Will do, speak soon." Swiping, I close out the call and lean my head back, letting out a groan. I rub my hand over my face. What the fuck do I do with this?

Bringing up the feed of the room across the landing, I see the beauty lying across the bed. She truly is a vision. There's a lump in my chest. This is who I've been searching for, the one I've longed to see all these years... how is it possible? If it wasn't for those eyes, I would never have recognized her at all.

She can't stay here, not after what she's been through. I'm just as bad as that son of a bitch... fuck!!

Pacing back and forth, I can't believe what I'm doing, what I've been doing, but fuck! A roar leaves me. I know the right thing to do. Yes, she has to leave, but now that I've had a taste there's no way I can let her go. Not. A. Fucking. Chance!

Mine. The question is do I let her know the truth?

CHAPTER 11
Meghan

I've been locked in this room for over a week, with only his voice to keep me company and the daily visits from Marco to drop me my meals. I'm going crazy.

Why am I even here? If he doesn't want to have sex with me and he doesn't need a fucking cleaner, then why? I'm sick of begging and pleading to be released; every attempt I've made to leave only leads to a shock. Every time I disobey any command is the same. My neck is sore from the onslaught.

I'm destined to be locked away and used for whatever men want to do to me. I don't know what I did in a previous life, but I sure as shit deserve to be treated like a fucking princess in the next… wait… that's it! Turning my head to the side, I look out to the balcony, the one I loved when I first came here. Now I've hardly been out there, choosing to sit in the far corner of the room and hiding on the shadows, hoping I'm out of his sights, yet longing for him to see me. This is so fucked up. I'm fucked up!

Placing my hands on the cold tiles, I get up from the floor. My body aches from the position I've been in for hours. Tugging at the hem of the t-shirt I'm wearing, trying to cover myself, I make my way to the stunning balcony. I want to hate it here, but I'm always at war with myself. Each day I sit, waiting for his voice to come through the speakers to tell me what to do.

I want to please him and disobey at the same time, thinking he will come and punish me or reward me, but nothing. Laughing at myself for how ridiculous I'm being, I head on out. I feel the warmth of the tiles on my bare feet, heating my body, and the sun on my face urges my head to tilt toward the sun.

Placing my hands on the balcony, I feel the peace that comes from being so far up and away from any other human beings. The property is closed off from any neighboring properties. Inhaling deeply, my mind goes blank. The peace takes over and a smile spreads across my face. This is it. I've found my inner peace, a place where I can be free. My foot stands on the bottom railing as I pull myself up and swing my leg across so I'm perched on top, feet dangling over the edge.

That's my life, always on the edge, but I feel nothing but peace. My hair blowing in the breeze, the sun shining on my face, I push myself forward as I let go of the balcony, exhaling as my hands release…

Arms wrap around my waist, pulling me back, gripping tightly. "What the fuck, what are you doing?"

He's here. I'm pulled in to a hard chest, and his sandalwood scent engulfs me. My pussy awakens instantly and a groan leaves me.

I go to push him away but he doesn't move an inch. "What are you doing here? You don't want me, please j..just let me go." I'm pleading with him, but my head is screaming for him to just hold me like this forever. What the fuck was I thinking; I don't want to die.

I get dizzy. It must be the adrenaline, of realizing what I just tried to do. Tears spring to my eyes. "I d..don't want to die." Tears fall from my eyes as my legs give way, but I don't fall as he has me wrapped in his arms. I feel like I am floating as the light from the sun fades away as I feel the softness of silky sheets touch my skin. His hand runs through my hair as his lips graze my head.

His breath touches my face as his tongue peeks out, licking my tears away. "Mine." The break in his voice is clear as his lips gently kiss my forehead. "You're all mine, always."

My eyes close as he pulls me into his hard chest. I feel safe, like this is where I am meant to be. I relax and fall into a restful sleep.

Waking in the morning, I know I am not in my usual room. I can feel something hard pressing into my back, my hands are resting on top of ones much larger than my own... it's him, and he's still here!

"Good morning, sugar." I can feel the vibrations of his voice along my back.

"Why am I here?" I almost whisper, afraid of the answer.

"The moment I set my eyes on you, I wanted you." His hand on my stomach turns me over so I'm flat on my back, his eyes staring into mine. "The moment I tasted you, I needed you, and the moment I sank into your tight wet cunt, you were mine. I am never going to get my fill of you, sugar." His breath tickles my neck as he licks along the column up toward my ear.

I feel his words in my core. I'm aching for him to touch me, to fuck me like he really does want to keep me. Yet I'm confused; he has changed. Is that because of yesterday or because of something else?

"What's changed? You've kept me locked up for almost two weeks now. Is it because of yesterday? Because if it i.." His finger rests on my lips to stop me from finishing.

"Yesterday was yesterday. I think today we start from fresh." A smile spreads across his face, lightening his eyes. It's breathtaking.

"What? How can we forget everything that's happened? You've collared me, shocked me, and kept me locked up. Why would you do that?" Raising to my elbows, I keep looking at him, demanding an answer.

"Don't you like the collar, sugar?" His finger traces along my jaw, down along my neck, and over the collar on my neck. I feel goosebumps forming as he goes and swallow, trying to gain moisture in my mouth which appears to have gotten as dry as the Sahara.

"I..I don't like being shocked." Tilting my head down, I avert my gaze from his.

"Oh, sugar, you know how to stop that, don't you?" I lift my eyes and see his gorgeous mouth smirking back at me. I choose not to answer.

His throat clears, making my eyes wander back, and he cocks his eyebrow.

I exhale. "I need to be a good girl." My teeth claw on my bottom lip, stopping myself from pouting.

"Good girl," he practically purrs. "I may have been a little hasty in locking you inside, so for that I apologize, sugar." I must look like a goldfish with my mouth opening and closing, not knowing what to say to his apology, when he winks at me.

This man is going to ruin me, and for the first time in my life, I don't think I am going to mind.

CHAPTER 12
Reed

Leaving her in bed was the last thing I wanted to do, but she needed rest after yesterday. Fuck, that was a wake up call! One I shouldn't have needed.

She deserves more than this life, more than me, but I'm a selfish son of a bitch who isn't letting her go, not now not ever.

Carlos will pay for what he's done to her, I can guarantee that.

How do I begin to explain who I am? All these years she has thought I'm dead, but here I am alive and well. This is not the reunion she'd have dreamt of, that's for sure.

Laughing to myself, I start the shower, dropping the joggers I had on last night. Stepping inside, waiting for the water to heat up to the temperature that eases my tension, the steam billows around me as the water pelts down onto my skin. Lifting my head up, I let the water cover my face and run down the hard expanse of my chest.

I hear the small patter of her feet before the coolness of the air that surrounds her when she enters the shower behind me. Her hands are soft as she gently touches my back.

I spin around to catch her off guard when my breath catches in my throat. She's kneeling before me, just inches away, and my cock twitches in anticipation.

I clench my jaw. "Sugar, you should be in bed resting." Her eyes linger on my hardening cock, and the tip of her tongue peeks out, running across her plump lips as she peers up at me.

"I'm not tired." Her hands softly move up my thighs. "I want to thank you." Leaning forward, I can feel her breath on my cock causing me to groan. "Please." Her voice is husky as she smiles up at me. I can't say fucking no.

"This is what you want, is it, sugar?" I run my hand over her head, feeling the softness of her hair between my fingers. "Tell me."

"I want to suck your cock." Her lips move in and out as she bites on them nervously.

"Show me what you've learned, sugar." Winking at her, I watch her swallow as she moves forward and runs her tongue along the shaft, swirling around the head and lapping up the salty precum that's leaking from the tip. Her hand moves up and starts to pump up and down, teasing me, while the other massages my balls. "Stop teasing me, sugar." I place my hand on the back of her head as she takes me down her glorious throat, straight down until I hit her gag reflex. She changes her breathing and I go further down… fuck. Her head bobs faster and faster, and the tears start running down her perfect face. I feel every moan she makes around my cock. I feel the tingling in my balls. Her hands let go and she rises slightly, her legs move like she's trying to get friction… my little firecracker is close.

I grab her hair, pulling her from my cock before I explode down her throat, she hisses from the pain and moans at the pleasure she gets from the feeling.

"As much as I want to come down that pretty little throat of yours, sugar, right now I want to come in that sweet little pussy of yours." My hands still in her hair and I push her face forward to the wall so that the water pounds down on her.

"Hands flat on the wall and push your ass out." I watch as she follows my command, my hand runs down her spin, finding its way to her puckered hole, and she jolts. Leaning forward, I whisper, "This will be mine too."

"You're fucking soaked." My hand roams back and forth, taking in her pleasure. "Does sucking my cock turn you on?"

"Mmm, fuck." Her breathing picks up as I start to finger fuck her, slipping two fingers inside. Keeping them where they are, I stop.

"Does it?" I feel her push back, trying to fuck my fingers.

"Y..yes, It d..does, please don't stop!" The begging from her pretty little mouth does things to me that I will never be able to understand, and I don't think I want to. She's perfection.

I feel her pussy start to grip my fingers. I withdraw slowly and line myself up and plunge in, making her scream at the sudden intrusion. I hiss at the tightness gripping my cock. I know I'm only going to last so long after having her mouth around me so I move my hand around and tease the sensitive bundle of nerves as I fuck her hard against the wall. My hand snakes up around her throat, squeezing hard until I see her eyes glaze slightly and I release, again and again until I feel her pussy clamp down and she screams out. I follow with a roar as my cock pulses, emptying my seed deep inside.

Pulling away, I watch as my seed spills out, running down the inside of her thighs. My mind wanders. She could leave, but she wouldn't if she was pregnant.

I drop to my knees and run my hands along her thighs, pushing my seed back inside her. She looks over her shoulder, her eyebrow raised.

"What are you doing?" Her feet shuffle around as she looks at me.

"You take all of me, sugar. I know you'd swallow it all for me, wouldn't you?" I raise my brow, smiling at her, and she nods at me. "I'm just helping you. I like knowing you're full of me, sugar." Pulling her in, I kiss her mound and my cock twitches like he's ready to go again. I can't resist; my tongue licks and teases around her lips, dipping down toward her entrance. Her hands grip my head. I can taste us both: her sweetness and a hint of salty... perfection.

Her hips move, and she lifts her leg and brings it up to my shoulder as she rides my face. Keeping hold of her as she takes what she needs, I move one hand down to my cock and start to jerk back and forth. Our moans are filling up the air, her legs grip my head, and I feel her wet heat soak my face, the shake in her legs as she comes down from her high.

Standing, I push her down to her knees. "Look at me." My hand works up and down my shaft, and her hands move up her body, touching her perky tits.

Her mouth pops wide open and her tongue sticks out and she winks. *What the actual fuck*! Cum spurts from my tip, coating her tongue and chest. She hasn't stopped looking at me. Closing her mouth, she licks her lips. Running her finger over her tits, smearing cum everywhere. Lifting her finger, she pops it in her mouth and sucks. With a pop, her finger comes out and she stands. "You taste so good, baby."

Seeing the twinkle in her eye, I reach for the shower head and we rinse down quickly in an almost freezing shower and get changed in to sweat pants and t-shirts. She looks adorable in them as they completely dwarf her, but I need her covered because we have things we need to discuss and I can't be distracted.

CHAPTER 13
Maghan

F ollowing him down the hallway, my eyes take in the surroundings. Ornate paintings line the walls leading to the open staircase. The concrete steps feel cool on my feet as I step leisurely down each one, my hand gliding down the black shiny banister.

I didn't get a good look when I first arrived, but down here there has to be a good ten rooms just as I glance around. God knows what they all are or why he even needs that many.

Walking through a side door, I take in everything. It's beautiful! The infinity pool glistens in front of me, overlooking the ocean and mountains, what a back drop!

He reaches out and takes my hand. I feel a shock and his eyes meet mine; he felt it too!

Before I can think anymore about that, he drops his gaze and pulls me along to the seating area. Surrounded by large potted plants in an array of colors, we sit under an umbrella to shade us from the mid-day sun. Marco appears from nowhere with a tray, bringing refreshments.

"Thank you, Marco. If we need anything else, I will call you." He nods at him and he leaves without a word.

"Ooookay, what's going on?" Releasing his hand, I lean forward on the cushioned chair.

Clearing his throat, he adjusts his chair, facing me directly. "*Hope*, what's my name?" His brow raises.

Shifting uncomfortably, I don't know what to say. Something is off here, and the way he said *my* name… What am I missing? A chuckle leaves me. "Mr. Reed?" The question is clear in my voice as I shrug my shoulders.

"No, sugar…*that's* what Marco calls me. My name is Reed. Do you know anyone else called Reed?" I swallow as his gaze stays fixed on me, like he is trying to see inside my mind.

My mind goes back ten years, thinking of my brother. *Well,* adopted brother Reed, but now isn't the time. He isn't here anymore; he can't help me. The only person I can rely on now is myself.

Swallowing nervously, I keep his eye contact. "Not that I can recall. Nice to meet you, *just* Reed." Tilting my head to the side, I offer my hand for him to shake, smirking at him as he narrows his eyes at me.

Slowly he reaches out and takes my hand in his. When he grips, I feel it in my core. "Likewise, Hope. It *is* Hope, right?"

Fuuuuck! My heart is racing; it's like I have a thousand butterflies in my chest fighting to get out. My palms are getting sweaty and my breathing is picking up; I have to control myself.

I make a noise that was supposed to be a laugh, but it comes out more like one of those honk honk horns clowns use. I am so screwed. He doesn't look angry, which is a plus, but what the actual fuck is going on here?

Feeling the blush on my cheeks, I look at him. "Of course, what else would it be?" *Why, why, why did I just ask that?*

"Sugar, you know what happens when you tell a lie?" His lips go into a thin line as his jaw clenches. I'm watching the muscles working when he taps the table to get my attention.

I sit quietly, thinking what to say or do next, not sure where this path will lead. Reed stands and joins me on the garden sofa. His hand reaches up and holds around my neck, his thumb running along the collar sitting so innocently there.

"I think you know, so tell me." His tongue peeks out and runs over his soft lips, ones that I can still remember how they felt touching my skin. Just the thought sends a shiver all over.

My eyes burn as I try to hold back the tears threatening to fall. I am at constant war with this man. I want to obey his every command, but my brain is fighting with me, telling me that this could be dangerous, real fucking dangerous. It looks like my body wins as I blurt out, "I'm sorry." More tears fall as I look over to the mountains, searching for something. I don't know what I am looking for, maybe a time where I don't live in fear for what happens when I am just me, just Maghan.

"You're safe here with me, you can tell me anything." Pulling me closer, I feel the warmth from his skin through his white t-shirt that moves with his muscles.

"My name is Maghan… C..Carter, I'm from New York." His breath catches and his jaw starts to work overtime. If he isn't careful, he'll need to replace a molar!

"Why are you here? How did you get here?" His forefinger lifts my chin to look at him, and my lips tremble as I fight to stop the tears from falling.

"I ran, okay. I got on a container and it ended up here. I didn't know where the container was going, I just thought it would be going to a different state!" Jerking my body backward to get away from him, his grip tightens. "Why do you want to know?" My hand lifts up in question, knocking the glass on the table to the floor. Heaving a sigh, I look back to Reed. "What do you want from me?"

"You. I want all of you, sugar." A smile fills his face. "I have some things you need to see but first, we need to go somewhere safe. I don't want you getting cut from that glass." He lifts me like I weigh nothing and we move back through the double doors to a room with a dark oak door to the left.

He places me down when we enter what appears to be his office. My eyes take in burnt orange walls, brown tiled floors, a large oak desk in the middle, with one of the strangest pictures I have ever seen mounted on the wall.

He starts to laugh at me when he catches my eyeline. "Beautiful, isn't it" I scrunch my face up and nod my head yes as he continues to laugh at me, while eyeing the painting of the horse with a tentacle cock.

There are papers neatly lined on his desk. I can see my name on the first one. Looking at him, I make my way over to it, picking it up. I sit in the leather chair in front of the desk and look up as Reed sits in the chair next to me. I start to flick through the folder when I land on a page that I have seen before but not for many years: my adoption paper. This one has our photos as children and an ache fills inside me as I see Reed...my brother.

"Wait, how do you have this? Did you know my brother?" Flicking the paper up, I show Reed the photo, and his laugh is dark as he looks back at me. "I do. It's been a long time, wouldn't you say, sugar?"

WHAT...THE...FUCK!

"Y..you're h..him." My mouth drops open. I can't see the resemblance; is this possible? Oh my god! I've fucked my brother!!

"I can hear you thinking from here, sugar. We aren't related." Standing, he grabs my chin and slams his mouth onto mine. I open automatically, my body taking over and letting him in instantly. His tongue slips in and he swallows my moan. I let the papers fall to the floor as I reach up to hold on when he steps back.

"Related or not, you're mine, sugar. Nothing will ever fucking change that."

"But you're my fucking brother. We fucked! Oh, my god!" I

shout, moving back away from him as I cover my face with my hands. How could this have happened? For so many years I have wanted to see Reed, I have wished for the moment that we come face to face again, but this… This is not a situation I ever thought I would be in.

How the fuck did I not know who he was? Reed is a common name, right? That can just be a coincidence. But how did I not notice anything else about him; it's not like I was a baby when he "died".

The more I look at him and the picture of Reed on the floor from ten years ago, all my memories come flooding back. Memories that I have tried to keep locked away.

Maybe I tried to ignore the obvious signs in front of me because of how he made me feel all this time and how I have longed to feel all these years…safe.

"How long have you fucking known?" I shout, looking at Reed, pointing my finger at him.

"Be very careful, sugar. I know you are shocked, so I will forgive your outburst," he says as he comes closer.

"Are you fu.. serious right now?" I question. Of course I choose to lose the curse word as I have an idea what his plan would be, and as much as part of me is on board with that, my brain is confused as fuck and he doesn't seem to give a shit.

"As a heart attack. It doesn't matter how long I have known. We are not blood related. I told you because I wanted there to be no secrets between us. This changes nothing between us," he tells me so matter of factly, I want to believe him.

CHAPTER 14

Reed

S tanding back, I can see the look of disbelief on her face. She's shocked, but I have to carry on. She needs to know everything.

One thing I have to get straight. She is mine, those adoption papers sealed it. The past is the past, and what we're dealing with now is the fall out from some of that, but we will. And payback is due.

"I need you to listen to me carefully, sugar. I know what you were told about me, and as you can see that was all a lie. I can also see that you didn't kill yourself either. Carlos wanted me out of the way for his own gain, and you were just an added bonus." Pacing my office, I can feel the anger rising inside at everything I know about what he did and how he used her over the years.

My cell vibrates, interrupting me. Carlos's name flashes over the screen.

"Boss," I grit out, trying to contain the anger and clenching my fists. Maghan stands to come over to me, but I lift my finger to my lips and place him on loud speaker.

"I'm coming over to see you. We have issues here, and I

need to lay low for a while. My cunt of a sister went rogue," he spits out.

"What the fuck are you talking about?" My hands rake through my hair; how he talks about Caitlin infuriates me.

"I sent her to the Riveria Mafia. All she had to do was gather information on shipping containers. I could have taken over the remaining parts of the East Side, take complete fucking control, and she had one job, one fucking job... the useless piece of shit!" I'm smiling as pride overtakes the anger I felt. Whatever she's done, she's really pissed him off. I listen to him rant and shout until he says something of interest.

"I've left her with Zeke. He's going to get the information we need out of her, by whatever way he has to. Last I heard, the little bitch was strung up, reeking of her own piss." His laugh comes through the line.

"When can I expect you, Carlos? I have things I need to attend to." I need to get hold of Sawyer to find out where Caitlin is and fast!

"I'll be there in a week or so. I can't fly. I need to stay out of sight, but nothing changes with the shipments. Keep them as they are." My eyes roll as he ends the call.

"You have to let me leave if he's coming here. I can't stay, he'll take me back with him!" She rushes over and grabs my hands in hers. "Please! You *have* to let me go."

"He won't touch you, you have to trust me on that. There's a lot Carlos doesn't know. These containers he's so worried about are full of people, mixed with product. At first I didn't know, not until recently. As for Carlos, he still thinks I don't know." I open up the drawer, taking out the files full of people he sent over. Some went back, some went on to the final destination for a better life in the countries I have contacts in and were unloaded with the product. "It can't continue, each week more and more were coming." Sitting in the chair, I look at her waiting, for her reaction. I can't let myself think how many people have gone through me without me realizing. If I hadn't been so fucked up, I could have done something about it sooner.

"So...what does he think happens?" Her brows lift in question.

"Look, Carlos doesn't care as long as he gets his money, and I have operations running here for other distributions. The containers are valuable and can be used for many different things, sugar, but what I won't tolerate is people. I thought I'd stopped it, but some still get through depending who he has working the docks. It's still in its infancy and not being in New York, I can't get everywhere...yet," I assure her.

"I think that's enough for today, I have things I need to sort out. Before you go and rest, I want you to think about something for me." Going toward her, I take her hands gently, bringing them toward my lips. "I would like you to speak to someone about yesterday and everything you've been through." My lips brush the back of her hands.

"I want to, I just don't know if I am ready. There's so much that I don't understand myself. How would I begin to explain any of this to someone else?" She doesn't sound sure in her response.

"Sugar, you trust me, don't you?" I ask her soothingly. Leaning down, I kiss her forehead and I know when she raises her head and nods that she will do as I have asked.

"It'll help," I assure her as I watch her turn and walk toward the door.

"Sure, sounds good." The door clicks as she closes it behind her.

My shoulders relax knowing she's going to speak to some-one. How we met wasn't conventional, but that wasn't why she broke. I will be here helping her with whatever she needs to become the warrior she is.

Swiping through my contacts searching for Sawyer, I hit call, talking before he speaks.

"I need you to locate Caitlin Russo, this takes priority over everything," I command.

"Hello to you too, boss." A chuckle fills the line, along with the tapping of a keyboard.

"This is important. I need information on the Riveria Mafia, what do you know?" I start rummaging papers, shoving the files back into my desk.

"The Don, Jax, he's a nasty motherfucker, but has several clubs. Can't say for sure what he's into, I'll need to dig deeper." Chewing fills the line and a pop, chew and pop.

"I'll send the info I have. I need her found and I want to contact her. I need to find a way without Carlos knowing. Call me." I sigh to myself when I realize I've done what pisses me off the most: hung up without saying anything. *What a dick*!

Leaning back in my seat, I blow out a breath, thinking of what the next couple of weeks will bring. I need Sawyer to get this information fast before Carlos gets here. Once that son of a bitch steps off that boat in Italy he sure as shit won't be returning to the States… not alive anyway.

The vibration from my cell takes me from my thoughts.

> Sawyer: Found their guy, reached out, should hear soon.

> Me: Great work

> Sawyer: Boss… Is this you?

> Me: Fuck off

> Sawyer: Thank god! I thought you'd been kidnapped.

> Me: :-/

CHAPTER 15
Maghan

W hat the fuck just happened? Leaving the room, my mind is all over the place. I have no idea what to think. I'm relieved that Reed is alive... who I thought was my brother didn't die. But the man standing there in front of me isn't him; to be honest I wouldn't have recognized him as the man I knew back then. He's hardened over the years.

I keep thinking about the brother I remember, but it's hazy. A lot has happened since then, none of it good.

Marco interrupts my thoughts on my way to the guest room.

"Miss! I'm sorry to bother you, but I have added some clothing to Reed's closet for you. Don't worry, you will be able to get some more items soon. It's just a few bits for now." Smiling, he turns and pushes a door that swings back and forth behind him. I'm left confused as I watch it swing.

He's moved my rooms and got me clothes. When did he do this?

I need to clear my head; there's so many things going through it at the moment I don't know where to start.

Firstly, Carlos will be here and that has my stomach in knots. I feel sick at the thought, but I do trust Reed—and that thought alone scares the hell out of me! I haven't known him that long, not really, and most of that time I've been locked in a bedroom!

Secondly, my feelings for Reed are stronger than what they should be. I want to be with him. I long for his touch, the craving for the pleasure and pain he delivers. Pushing me to limits I didn't know existed within myself makes me yearn for this Reed even more.

Thirdly, I'm scared of going through with the therapy I promised I'd do. What if he decides I'm too fucked up for him and wants me to leave after all this time of trying to keep me here? My heart aches just thinking he could push me away.

I start looking through the side of the closet I've been allocated and see there's some swimwear, and decide that taking a swim should help with clearing my mind. Throwing the joggers and t-shirt into the hamper, I change quickly into the strappy red two piece. I mean, it doesn't leave much to the imagination, but it at least covers most of me. Plus it's not like anyone will see me.

Grabbing a towel, I head back to the pool and place my towel on one of the sun beds. I dive in and start laps. I stop counting after twenty and see a figure waiting for me at the end of the pool. My body burns and aches; I've pushed myself to the limit. My mind is clear from the mess that's going on around me, and I feel free.

My head bobs up at the feet of the figure, and realize it's Reed watching me after I raise my hand above my eyes to shield the sun from blinding me.

"Looking good, sugar, feeling better?" He bends down, placing his elbows on his thighs.

"I am. I needed to clear my mind; exercise helps." Swimming away from him to the steps, I pull myself out of the pool.

Looking over my shoulder, I smile at him as he stands and walks over to me. My eyes drop to his sweatpants and I can see the outline of his manhood tenting his pants. My core aches, and I bite down on my lip, trying to withhold a groan.

Strolling past me, he sits on the sun bed. My stomach twists at the rejection I feel; I thought he was coming to me. I wanted him to because I need him.

Breathing in, I go over and pick up the towel and wrap it around me. I clench my jaw, the mantra chanting in my head... do not show you're bothered is on repeat. I turn to go back to the villa as Reed's hand takes hold of my wrist.

"Where you going, sugar?" The growl flows through my body, hitting all the right spots.

"I need a shower." I raise my eyebrow, still trying to pretend I'm not affected my him when I can feel my body betray me.

"Come sit with me." He tugs me closer.

"Do I have a choice?" I shoot back at him as I land on his lap.

"Sure you do, but we both know you'd rather be here with me than in the shower alone," he purrs, his hand running up and down my spine.

He inches me up and pulls down his sweatpants, freeing his hardened cock.

"Take what you want, sugar. You know what we are to each other, you know you're mine." Reaching out, his hand runs along my cheek. "I trust you. I'm all yours, too, I'm all in... forever." His arms go above his head and he clasps his hands together, resting his head back.

Looking around, I'm unsure. I know what I want... him.

I have no other feelings toward him other than the ones of want and need, and I don't feel bad about that. Maybe I should but that's something to discuss later... maybe.

He's trusting me to take charge, which is huge. Maybe he really does feel the same if he is being vulnerable like this with me.

Either way, I am not letting this opportunity pass me by!

I stand next to him, sliding my hands along his legs to reach for band of his sweats and pull them all the way down.

Straddling his legs, I lift his t-shirt so he is naked beneath me. I lean forward, running my tongue along his stubbled jaw, and whisper in his ear.

"No touching until I say so." Moving back, I wink at him as my hands roam his torso, my head dipping kissing his neck, my tongue making its way down further and further past the ridges of his muscles, feeling them clench beneath me as I go.

Licking and sucking his balls as I take them in the palm of my hand, my eyes meet his as I smirk. I see him wrestle with keeping his hands to himself; he wants to take control. Precum leaks from his tip, and my tongue swirls around, lapping it up, earning a groan from him.

"Fuck, sugar…suck it, take my cock in that pretty little mouth of yours." I can hear how on edge he is, and I love that I can do this to him. I feel confident, wanted.

"That's what you want? You want me to take your big hard cock in my mouth and suck you dry?" I ask as I lick the length of his shaft.

Raising to my knees, I pull the strings of my bikini and let the bottoms drop free and do the same to the top. I watch as his head drops back and he curses.

My hand drops between my legs. Feeling how wet I already am, I start to run my hand up and down. I allow myself time to enjoy the sensations of my soft hand toying with my sensitive bud, then I stop and move my hand away and run it along his lips.

"I'm running out of control, sugar. I need you. You taste so fucking good." He grabs me and kisses me passionately, and we start to battle. Our teeth clash. I push back, knowing where this will end, and knowing I don't care. This is my time.

"Tut, tut, tut. Patience." I smile at him. He shakes his head, narrowing his eyes with a smirk.

I hover my pussy over his cock and start to rub my juices along his shaft. I start slow and my body starts to chase the feeling that's building inside. I get faster, and my nails dig into his shoulders. My moans are breathy, and I can feel my nipples grazing his chest as I move back and forth.

"Ah fuck, sugar, you're killing me." His hands are gripping my ass, moving me faster, urging me on.

"Ooo ffuck," I stutter as I let go.

"Jesus, my cock's drenched, baby." His breath is heavy on my neck.

I lift up slightly and move my hand so I can position him at my entrance, and in one motion I take him. I let out a moan that's half pleasure and half pain as I feel his cock stretching me. I don't give myself time as I start to move up and down.

"Fuck me, please, I need you," I beg him.

He meets me thrust for thrust. The pain morphs into pleasure as his hand moves to pinch my sensitive bud. His mouth finds my nipple and he sucks and nips hungrily. I'm so close.

"Reed, fuck...don't stop please, I'm so close," I beg.

He doesn't say anything. I feel vibrations on my nipple as he grunts, and his grip tightens on my hips as his thrusts get faster and faster. My back arches as I scream his name, and that's his undoing.

"Fuck!" His voice is gruff as I feel his seed filling me up completely.

I fall onto him, my body spent, neither of us moving. His length is still positioned inside me.

"Now we have that settled, sugar, I think we can move on from here." His lips press against my forehead as I bury my head into his neck, inhaling our mixed scents.

I've longed for this feeling of being safe, being accepted, the feeling of love and *hope*.

CHAPTER 16

Reed

Two weeks Later…

Containers come and go. There's no sign of anything that shouldn't be on there, which makes me wonder if something has happened back in New York.

I've been checking every container myself, and all we get is the usual: coke and guns.

Every time I stand and watch as the men he sends get off the container and load up the fishing boats one by one, seeing them sail off to their final destinations.

This morning's shipment is a surprise. One I've been expecting and preparing for, but seeing Carlos step out of the container, I wasn't expecting to feel as calm as I do now. Pulling my shoulders back, I stride over and greet him, nodding my head to show respect—*that he doesn't deserve!*

"Boss. I trust you had a pleasant journey?" Raising my hand, he takes it in his, pulls me in, and slaps my back with his free hand.

"Reed, you handsome motherfucker, this Italian sun has

worked wonders for you. You're looking good." His lips lift in a slimy smirk. He hasn't changed. His hair is slicked back, he has dark soulless eyes, and his designer suit is dirty from the container.

"I need a shower and a drink, then I can go through the details of the little issue my cunt of a sister has created." He sneers as he walks up the pier. "Also, I have a lot of stress I need to work out. Call someone in." Turning to look at me, he winks. "You know what I mean." My hands clench together inside my gray slacks; this guy makes me sick!

Back at the house, Carlos heads for the guest house out the back. It's a building that we never use, but Marco made it up for his stay. I watch from the pool as he follows Marco down there. I have set up cameras so I can watch what he does. I don't want any surprises and I don't want anything to happen to Maghan. I'm already pissed she can't use the pool while he's here. It's become a daily ritual and she's been following it regularly; it helps her relax.

Sawyer has been blowing my phone up. We know what Carlos tried to do to Caitlin, but thankfully Jax got to her in time, and she's now recovering at his home. I need to find out how much he knows. Zeke is no longer alive, but I'm not sure if he's aware of that yet. I sent a message to Caitlin assuring her I will make this right.

And I will, but for now that's all I'll send her. I think Jax may want in on my next plan so I will need to tread carefully, but if she trusts him and he saved her life, then I know I at least owe him.

Vibrations alert me of a message taking me from my thoughts. Sawyer's name appears on my screen.

"What do you have?" I get to the point.

"Caitlin received and listened to the message. It appears she's open to communication; they haven't closed the line." Tapping continues from his end.

"Great, I need you to message Jax. I don't want Caitlin

involved in this just yet, not until I know exactly how she is."
My thoughts go to the young girl I left. I can't believe what she's
been through because of the monster at the bottom of my garden.

"What do you want me to send? I have the file up now." His
constant blowing of bubbles and chewing eases me rather than
annoying me like it used to.

"Jax, I don't know you well, but what I know is you saved
one of the people I love most in this world. For that I will be
forever thankful. I *am* the head of the Russo Mafia and Carlos
doesn't know I know this. I will be eliminating him and invite
you to join in the happy occasion." I sigh. "I think that will do
for now. Keep comms open and add an RSVP."

Sawyer's laugh fills my ears. "Boss, fuck! I love it. It's done.
As always, I'll keep you posted."

"Great, thanks." I smile as I wait for him to hang up. There's
a first time for everything.

I linger, looking at Carlos move around in the guest house as
the sun sets behind it. Sending that message was a weight lifted,
an olive branch so to speak. I hope that communications between
us can remain open and, once we settle this business with Carlos,
we can make arrangements for our futures which I think can be
beneficial to all of us.

It doesn't take me long to get back in the villa. I know where
Maghan will be, but first I need to get everything in order for
when Jax and hopefully Caitlin arrive.

Picking up my phone, I call Marco and have him set up the
rooms on the ground floor at the back of the villa, plus a couple
extra just in case Jax decides to bring any of his men. I know I
would in his position.

"Oh, and Marco, send Lolita to my office when she arrives,
please." This is perfect; my hand runs across the shiny necklace
and a smile fills my face.

Knock, knock

Making my way to the sound, I unlock the bolt and open the
door. Lolita is standing, waiting for me to invite her in. Her

ponytail is pulled tight to the top of her head, bright red locks flowing down to her waist. Her thin ruby lips smile at me. Her tongue runs over her lips, which does nothing for me.

"Come in and sit." I gesture to the chair. Her eyes narrow at my request. It's unusual, I admit, but times change, things change and so, it would seem, I have changed.

"I would like for you to do me a favour. You would be rewarded well…when you succeed." I go around the desk and sit opposite her, maintaining eye contact.

"What do you want me to do?" I like her confidence. I have faith she can succeed in this, she has to!

"I want you to spend the night with my visitor in the guest house, and I want you to secure this around his neck." Passing over the necklace, she takes it from me. Her eyes light up when she sees the diamond sitting in the middle.

"This is not a necklace you want to keep, trust me on that." I raise my brow as I stand and go over and sit on the desk in front of her so she has to raise her head to look at me.

"Do you think this is something you can do?" My hands grip the desk, waiting for her response.

"How much?" she asks.

"Five hundred thousand euros, in cash." I hear her gasp.

"Okay, I will do it. When will I get my money?" The request is urgent; there isn't much you can't get people to do for money.

"When it is secure around his neck, text me." Rising from the desk, I open the door, looking over at her and smiling. "Have a lovely evening, Lolita."

CHAPTER 17

Reed

I haven't been able to go back to our room all night. I have to make sure he is secure first. I watched Lolita strut over to the guest house then knock on the door; ever since then I have sat in my office, watching out of the window.

I open the top buttons of my shirt, waiting and watching my phone on the table in front of me.

I swirl the crystal glass, listening to the ice gently tap against the sides and watching the clear liquid swish round and around. Glancing at the bottle, I smile when I see the gift that Carlos purchased for me. Kors vodka has to be one of the smoothest I've ever tasted. It's filtered through champagne limestone and infused with 24-karat gold flakes. The bottle itself is a work of art, encased in a gold-plated suit with a leather label... perfection.

Maybe a little early for celebrating, but cracking open this bottle that's worth just over twenty thousand euros feels right for what I'm hoping is a success.

I like the taste of success, but I'm eager to get down to business. Reaching for my phone, I call Sawyer, who answers on the first ring.

"Hey, any news back from Jax?" I need him to respond. If tonight goes as planned, I don't want to keep him here for long if I can help it.

"Yes, but short and sweet. I was just in the process of messaging you. He said that he would be delighted to join, when?" The chew and pop come through the line, waiting for my response.

"Message him and tell him to leave asap, I have rooms set up for him. Tell him I'll be expecting him." The smile on my face spreads; it feels like everything is coming together slowly.

"Sure thing, boss, I'll confirm the response." He's tapping away on his keyboard.

"Great, then..." I don't get to finish before he interrupts me.

"We have a response." He chuckles. "It appears someone is eager, they've said we will see you soon."

"Perfect, see you later," I say before cutting the call.

The pieces are finally coming together. I just have to be patient for a little while longer and then I'll have control over Carlos. I can't wait to discuss with Jax and Caitlin about what we plan to do with him.

The hours go by slowly and dusk turns to dawn as I watch, waiting. The sun pops up above the sea, sparkling and bringing with it a new day, a new host of opportunities. Today is the day where everything starts to change.

Laughing to myself, I drag my hand over my face, feeling the stubble that's grown. Thinking how much I miss my little firecracker, the need to wake up with her snuggling next to me every day is a foreign concept, but one I wouldn't change for the fucking world. I would trade everything I have for her, do everything I can in my power to keep her happy and safe. She's mine... forever.

My phone lights up on the table as I look up and see Lolita leaving the guest house quietly.

> Lolita: Done, he's asleep.

> Me: Good, money will be wired later once I can see it works correctly.

> Lolita: You said I'd get it when it was done.

I look up and see her glaring at the window of my office. I lift a shoulder and reply.

> Me: You'll get your money, be patient.

> Lolita: What choice do I have?

I know she isn't really asking me a question, so I pocket my phone and leave the office and head down to the guest house. My footsteps are light since I'm trying to keep my presence unknown.

I lock the doors from the outside and have already secured the windows. For now that's as safe as it can be. All the keys are in the main building so he won't be able to leave through the doors, and the windows can't be broken—not without me noticing first.

Rushing back to my office, I pull out my laptop and bring up the live feeds to the rooms to the guest house. I can see him still sleeping. I lean back in my chair, hearing the strain my weight has on it, as I put my hands behind my head in a stretch, smiling at the situation. So far so good!

I tap on the keyboard and bring up the camera I installed in the main bedroom. I see Maghan stirring so I text Marco and ask him to fetch her coffee and pastries.

I hit the mic. "Good morning, sugar." I watch as her head spins around the room, her eyes narrow.

"I thought we spoke about this." She pushes herself so she's leaning up against the headboard.

I chuckle. "Now, now, you didn't think I could leave you alone, did you?"

"You're only in your office, Reed!" she accuses.

"I know, but I can't keep an eye on you from in here. I want to keep you safe, sugar." I drop my tone, feeling my cock twitch as the cover drops to show her tits. Fuck! I can't get enough of this woman.

"Fine, but they have to go when this is over." She crosses her arms, and the sheet lifts back to cover her beautiful tits.

"Marco will be up soon with your breakfast. I want to see what you wore to bed last night." I put my hand over my cock and adjust my hardening length.

"I didn't wear anything." Her eyes cast downward.

"Don't be shy, baby, show me." I unfasten my button and lower the zipper on my slacks, pulling out my cock.

She drops the sheet and looks around the room. "Where's the camera?"

"Don't worry about that. I want to see you pleasure yourself, baby." My thumb runs over the top of my cock, rubbing in the precum I've already leaked.

Her head tips back and her eyes close. I watch as her hand teases over her hardening nipples, her fingers pinching and pulling as she gasps each time. Her hips begin to move on their own.

My jaw clenches as I watch her pleasure herself. I can hear how wet her pussy is. I urge her on as I jerk long and hard, looking at everything I want.

"I need to come, Reed, please, please can I come?" She's so fucking good. I love hearing her beg. I am so close, seeing her come undone will be it for me. Imagining her pussy clenching around my cock, her juices running down my shaft and covering my balls...fuck!

"Such a good fucking girl! Yes, come, come for me. I want to hear you call my name." My voice is labored.

Watching her come is something else. I follow, making a mess everywhere, but I couldn't give a shit!

"You're so fucking beautiful, baby," I tell her as she lays spread out on the bed.

She looks around, trying to find my voice, and brings herself to her knees in the middle of the bed. Running her fingers between her slit causes her to shudder. Her fingers come to her mouth as she sucks them clean one by one, looking in the direction she thinks I am at.

"Mmm. I taste so good, but we taste better together." A smirk forms on her face as she falls back on the bed and pulls the sheet back over her.

"Such a naughty girl, sugar, trying to tempt me when I have things to do" I purr.

Giggling, she covers her face and a knock on the door has her jumping back as Marco enters with her breakfast.

"Have a good day, sugar, be good!" I say as I tap out a text asking Marco to bring me a suit from my closet.

I flick to the screen as I check on Carlos and see he is still sleeping, which is good. I shouldn't have got distracted, but she's too tempting.

Marco comes in with my clothes and breakfast. I only have a short period of time before Carlos wakes, so I make use of the time and head to the downstairs shower room and get washed, skipping shaving to save time.

Unlocking the office door, I glance at the monitor and see movement. A smile spreads across my face… show time. I press the mic giving me access to the guest house.

"Good morning, Carlos, sleep well?"

"What the fuck? Why am I locked in? And what the fuck is this fucking thing strapped around my neck?" he shouts into the room.

"Patience, Carlos. Patience."

CHAPTER 18

Reed

Watching as Carlos paces round and around is satisfying as fuck. He's clawing at his neck, trying to release the collar. He has zero chance of removing it, but it's fun watching him try. Some would say I'm a cruel bastard, but others would say he deserves everything he gets.

I let the day pass, keeping an eye on the screen, as his anger rises and he starts to trash the room. Spittle flies from his mouth as his screams get louder, and he's smashing everything in sight.

"Come on, Carlos." My voice is even. "I think it's time to calm down. You're only wasting your energy, energy that you'll need." I chuckle as I watch his face redden.

"You'll be so fucking sorry when I get out of here, Reed, you mark my words," he shouts.

"You make the foolish assumption that you will be getting out... *alive.*" My tone deepens as anger seeps in.

"There is no way you can do this to me. What the fuck do you want?" He perches himself on the end of the messy bed.

I look around the guest house room. The kitchenette has been destroyed, the island clear of anything it had on it the night before. The dining table has been tossed over and the chairs thrown across into the small living area where the black leather sofa has been pushed at an angle, ruffling the rug beneath it.

Carlos is losing it slowly. His usually neat black hair is a mess, and he's sitting in his boxer shorts, elbows on his knees. It's truly a sight I will remember.

"Honestly, I want you to pay for what you've done. But now you wait. I don't have the time to go through everything. You've been fucking me over for ten years, so I think you can wait on me for a change. Now that I know what you've been doing, things are going to be different. It's my game now, Carlos, and my rules," I spit.

I decide to leave Carlos alone for a while. I want him to be alone with his own mind, thinking of what it could be that he has done. I know for sure that he has no idea that I know that Maghan is alive, but he has done a lot of things over the years and kept me at arm's length. Now I'm the one holding the leash.

A few hours pass and I check in with Marco, wanting to make sure that he has transport ready. The walk to the front isn't far, but I want to be there to greet and pick up my guests. I want as few people seeing them as possible... for now.

The black SUV is out the front with its tinted windows, perfect for what I will be needing it for.

"Hey." Her voice is soft but it makes the hair on the back of my neck stand on end, causing a shiver to run down my spine. God, I want her so fucking badly.

"You shouldn't be out here, sugar, it's not safe." I turn around and look at her standing in the doorway. I clench my jaw as I look at her head to toe, dressed only in one of my pale blue dress shirts.

She lowers her head, causing her luscious brown hair to fall forward to cover part of her face, and her cheeks flush. Her arms cross as if she wants to cover herself and she lifts one finger to her mouth and chews gently as if she's nervous.

"Especially dressed like that. What do you want, sugar?" I walk toward her, placing my hands in my pockets, the only way I'm not going to grab her and fuck her against the wall right now. I take some deep breaths as I close in on her. Her citrusy scent envelopes me, her hands reach for my shoulders as she stands on her tiptoes and leans into me, and I feel her warm breath along my jaw.

"I want you, I need you…please." Her tongue licks the lob of my ear, sucking it between her beautiful lips, and she groans softly.

My hands are out of my pocket fast. One grips her neck and pushes her against the door frame, another groan leaving her parted lips. My cock twitches at the sound.

"I want you, too, sugar, but this isn't safe and you're pushing me to the fucking edge." Pulling her bottom lip in between my teeth, I bite down as I watch her squirm, rubbing her thighs together. I can smell her arousal. It's like a red flag to a bull.

Letting my hand drop from her neck, I pull her behind me as I bend down and lift her over my shoulder. She squeals and a giggle leaves her which brings a smile to my face. God, that sound. I would burn the world down to only hear her happy, to keep her happy. I would give her anything she asks for, and I think she knows this now. I'm in all the way. Spinning round, I head for the stairs, taking two at a time, listening to them creak as we go.

I kick the door open and slam it closed, making sure to lock it behind us. I can't risk anything, not while he is here. He may be locked up, but I won't gamble anything when it comes to her.

Tossing her on the bed, the shirt she's wearing rises and I see that my fire cracker left the room without wearing any panties. Her arms lay flat on the bed and her brown locks fan out above her head.

"You're beautiful, you know that?" Stalking toward her, my weight tilts the mattress as I crawl toward her.

"You've been a naughty girl, sugar." I smile to myself as I

see the sparkle in her eyes. She knew what she was doing today, and she now has what she wants, but I am going to make sure the outcome will make her remember not to put herself in danger just so she gets what she wants.

Running my hands up her bare legs, I look at her glistening pussy, her body writhing as I continue my exploration. Grabbing hold of the pale blue shirt, I rip it open, hearing the tiny buttons clatter across the tiled floor. Her gasp fills my ears while the pebbled peeks of her tits grab the attention of my eyes.

Dipping my head, I bite down on her dusky pink nipple. Her hands land on either side of my head, her nails running back and forth, gripping my hair and pulling me closer while her pussy rises up, trying to grind herself against me.

My cock is pressing against the fly of my slacks. I fight the urge to free myself.

One of my hands goes around her throat while the other makes its way to heaven, her plump lips pop open in the perfect o.

I whisper, "You're soaked. Is this all for me, sugar?" My mouth is close to her ear, and I see the goosebumps appear all over her body.

"Ah fuck, yes, just you, please, stop teasing me." I love it when she starts to beg.

I slide three fingers in without warning and her scream turns to a moan, her hips now trying to take more than I'm offering.

"Tut tut tut," I whisper in her ear.

I continue to finger fuck her while teasing her breasts. I feel her pussy grip my fingers and remove them, hearing her whimper.

"No, please, I'm so close, please," she begs.

I bring my fingers to her lips, tracing her plump bottom lip with my forefinger.

"Suck." Shoving the digit inside and feeling her warm tongue dance around my finger has us both ready to explode. Her hand goes toward her pussy, but I grab her wrist.

"I don't think so, baby. The only one that gets to make you come... is me." Leaning down, I suck in her bottom lip, and my moans mirror hers.

I take her to the edge over and over. That's when I see and hear it; tears start to run down her cheeks. She's breaking right beneath me and it's fucking beautiful.

"I'm s..sorry, I won't do it again." Her voice is broken up with her crying.

She looks stunning, laid bare, her pussy dripping for me, tears running down her blushed cheeks. I wish I could take a picture of this moment.

"What's that?" Looking at her, I raise my brow.

"I won't leave the room when you tell me it's not safe," she rushes out.

"Good girl," I praise and softly kiss her lips.

I reach the button and fly, releasing my raging hard on. Breaking the kiss, I bend to remove my slacks.

"Please. I need you, I want to feel you inside me." She turns on her side facing me, throwing her leg over me so that we're nose to nose.

She leans over me and straddles me, her face still damp with tears. Her pussy strokes my cock, soaking me from base to tip, mixing our juices.

Her hand reaches down and guides me to her entrance, and she takes me in one thrust. Watching her face as it tinges with the pain and eases with the pleasure that follows, I wait for her to ride me fast. I know she's aching for release. Fuck, so am I, but my little fire cracker has other ideas.

Slowly she rises and falls, up and down. Her nails break the skin on my chest, causing me to hiss.

That doesn't break her torturous rhythm. She gradually speeds up, her palm gliding to my neck, toward my jaw, and her soft moans and gentle whimpers are a fucking symphony.

"Reed, ah fuck, I'm going to come." She shudders slightly, and I feel the pulse around my cock.

"Come for me, sugar." I take her lips and swallow her moans and we make love, both finding our release—something which I never thought I'd ever do… make love.

Her head drops to my shoulder. "I love you." Her voice is soft.

"I love you, too, sugar." My heart is full for the first time in a long fucking time.

Now I just have to deal with Carlos, then who knows what can happen. Turning my head, I look down at Maghan. She's my future. Fuck, she's my life.

CHAPTER 19
Meghan

Two weeks have passed since I left the room. He visits me everyday, but we don't sleep in the same bed.

I don't know what's happening, but I know Carlos is here and I don't like it. It's like he still has a hold over me, and that gives me a sinking feeling.

Something happened to stop Jax coming over from New York. I don't know what it was, but it had to be fucking important. I can feel the tension oozing out of Reed. He wants to end this as much as I do, but this guy has to be here.

I sink into the plush love seat that he had delivered to our room after I moaned at being kept locked inside with only the bed and the balcony chairs to sit on, and as luxurious as they are, I love to curl up on here and read smutty books on my phone.

Freeing my mind, I lose myself in a dark romance about a kickass woman who falls for a badass biker who's dark, dirty and dangerous. I smile to myself, thinking how he's pretty much everything your parents would tell you to avoid and exactly who you shouldn't want but man, the connection they have—I feel it in my core.

I read on. As I get to the juicy bits, my heart beats faster as I read her describing his pierced cock. I mean, I have an idea what that would look like but a google search never hurt, right?

My eyes widen as I scroll, looking at the piercings and imagining how they'd feel inside me. I wonder if Reed would get his done for me. My hand raises as I tap my forefinger on my lip, pondering how I can ask him.

His deep husky voice makes me jump when it comes through the speakers.

"You're deep in thought, sugar. What are you reading? I thought those *romance* novels of yours were supposed to help relax you."

I place my hand on my chest and gasp dramatically. "They do, and they *are* romance. They're just a little spicy, is all."

"Okay, if you say so. I have a surprise for you. I know you've hated being locked away, and I haven't been too happy about it either, so I wanted to make it up to you. But you have to promise that you will only use the guest room and this bedroom and not venture out anywhere else." His voice is stern and actually, I really fucking like the sound of it. It does something to me when he gets all bossy and demanding.

"Yes, I promise." I just want out of this room, to be honest. I've only seen three people these past couple of weeks. Suzi, my new therapist, who visits everyday. It's some kind of intensive therapy and I'm really enjoying it. At first I just thought she was stuffy, I mean who dresses in a trouser suit... in Italy in the summer! But she's really nice. Marco who brings me food, and of course Reed.

"Okay, I'll be up shortly. I have a few things to take care of and I will show you." I can hear the smile in his voice, and it makes my chest ache. I love hearing him that way. When Carlos is out of the way, hopefully we can spend time just being us, rather than having to spend time here and there. I can't lie; I love the idea of him watching me. I never know when he is or isn't, which is sexy as fuck.

I sit up, swiping off of the page I was viewing and rising to my feet.

"I'll get ready. I can't wait." Smiling, I look up over to the corner of the room. I assume that's where the camera is, but who knows. I blow a kiss in to the direction I think he's at.

Since I've not been able to go out, I've been able to order clothes online. Reed insists that I need to order more, but I'm already taking up a quarter of the closet space as it is.

I sit on the gray stool in the middle of the closet and look at my options. It's a little overwhelming in a good and bad way. I've never had this before, all these options, but I want to make sure I have something nice on, especially as I know I'll be seeing him.

I change into a beautiful pale green summer dress with a free flowing skirt that falls just above my knees. It really brings out the tan I've gotten since I've been here. The back falls low so I forgo wearing a bra. My hand reaches for some white lace panties when I think back to my book. Laughing, I remove my hand and choose to leave those behind too.

I've been waiting an hour and he hasn't arrived. I've been pacing the room, getting more and more impatient, when I hear the door unlock. Rushing over, I pounce on him as soon as he appears.

"Where have you been? I've been ready for ages." My arms snake around his waist, pulling him closer, feeling his hard chest against my now-hardening nipples. How just being in his presence and inhaling his masculine scent does this to me, I will never understand and I don't care. I've spoke to Suzi about my feelings for Reed and how intense they are, and we've agreed that I should embrace what I feel, so that's exactly what I'm going to do... literally!

His hands run up my arms as he pushes me back gently. "Looks like someone's missed me." Leaning forward, his lips brush mine softly, almost teasingly.

"You know I have." I can't hide the sadness that I feel,

knowing that these moments we spend together are short so we need to make the most of them.

"Me too, sugar, but it's not for long now, I promise." He takes my hand. "You ready for your surprise?" His lips rise in a smirk. Turning to leave the room, he looks back and winks at me.

That one wink is like lighting a match; my insides are on fire. Pressing my legs together, I nibble on my lip and nod my head yes, feeling the blush rise on my cheeks.

Chuckling at me, knowing exactly what he's doing, he crosses the hallway toward the guest room. There are several other rooms that I still need to look at yet, but so far I've only seen our bedroom and the guest room upstairs… wait, *our* room! Shaking my head, I stand next to him as he drops my hand, taking the key out of his pocket.

"You ready, sugar?" His brow raises.

"Yes. Yes, I've been ready for hours," I tell him, urging him to hurry up.

The door unlocks, and he pushes it open and moves out of the way for me to enter. Stepping forward, I stand in the entrance and stop still. My mouth drops open and I look from left to right, taking in what he's done.

The room does not look the same. All the furniture has been removed and the walls are covered from top to bottom with bookshelves, a ladder attached so I can reach the top.

A red circle chair filled with white cushions is placed in the middle facing the balcony, with a blanket draped over the arm.

"You can go in, you know." His hand nudges the bottom of my back and urges me in.

Not all the shelves are full, but some of the books I've mentioned are sitting on the shelves. I can feel my eyes burning but I'm fighting so the tears don't fall. This is amazing. I don't know what to say.

My hand glides over the softness of the blanket draped over the chair as I make my way to the ladder, and it really does slide across the floor. God, I feel like Belle in *Beauty and the Beast*!

Swinging around, I look at Reed and he's leaning against the doorframe with his hands in the pockets of his black slacks. The top few buttons of his white shirt are open. After all these years, this is it. Everything I've been through was for this moment here.

"Reed, I don't know what to say. This is so thoughtful, it's amazing. I love it so much!" Going over to him, my hands brush over the stubble on his face. "Thank you." I kiss his lips softly. "This means so much to me." I feel the warm tear escape and trickle down my cheek, but his hand rises and his thumb catches it before it falls.

"For you, sugar, anything." He lifts me up like I weigh nothing and carries me over to the ladder, placing me down, turning me to face forward, my back pressing into his front.

Moving my hair away from my neck, his warm breath flows across my ear. "Now, choose a book, baby. I want to hear you read to me."

"What?" I spin my head around to look at him, seeing the smirk on his face. "Why?"

"Pick good, baby. I'm about to show you how much better it all feels in real life." His hands roam down my body, making me squirm under his touch.

Grabbing one of my favourites, I open up a random page and begin to read. This is one that is pure smut from start to end. As I start reading, he drops to his knees. His hands grab my ass, squeezing and pulling me toward him.

Whimpering between reading, I break off every so often when his tongue starts teasing my puckered hole. His fingers are relentlessly toying with my sensitive bud, dipping down toward my entrance.

"There's not a single thing I wouldn't give you, sugar." I feel the vibrations of his voice on my pussy which make me groan. "I want everything from you. You're mine, there isn't anything I wouldn't do for you." I hear his zip sliding down as he pulls my hips backward and in one thrust I'm full, in the most beautiful way.

Moaning at the intrusion, the book slips from my hand, landing on the floor with a thud.

"Choose another." His voice is labored as his thrusts get faster and faster. The slap of our skin and the feel of his hand nipping and squeezing my tits are so erotic.

I reach out and pick the first book I can reach and start again. I struggle to form the words, not taking in what I am reading; all I can do is feel the building orgasm that's coming.

"I..I c..can't, Reed, please, I need to come," I stutter as my words are failing me.

"Such a good fucking girl… Come for me, sugar." His voice sounds like he's purring as I explode. He follows me with a roar, my name falling from his lips as he fills me with his warm seed.

Turning to face him, finding his lips, I kiss him softly. "Fuck, I love your surprises."

CHAPTER 20

Reed

Fuck...We need to get this Carlos shit sorted out and soon!

Every time I leave her it's harder than the time before. If you'd have told me six months ago that I'd be a one woman man, I'd have laughed in your face. But now, there's no way I could be with anyone else. It's like she was made for me, like I breathe just for her, my heart beats just for her, everything I do now is because of her.

Jax is finally on his way and will be here soon. I cannot fucking wait. After ten years the past can finally be put to bed.

I've been monitoring Carlos over the past two weeks and he isn't doing too well, which is great, but I want to get to him before he truly breaks by himself. I'll have to see what I can do about that.

Sitting in the chair in my office, I see he's sitting on the floor in the guest house, so I turn the mic on.

"Ah, Carlos, how are you?" I keep my tone upbeat and friendly.

His head starts looking around the room, searching for where the speakers could be. *He'll never find it.*

"Reed, is that you?" He starts running his hands through his hair nervously. He's gone through stages, and I'm sure anger will be back shortly.

"Yes. What are you doing? Why aren't you dressed?" I question him, playing with his mind.

"Why would I? I'm locked inside, you locked me in here!" he shouts, standing and throwing the bedsheet on the floor.

Laughing loudly through the mic, it echos. "What are you talking about, Carlos? You are locked in there because you snapped the key in the lock. How much coke did you take?"

He rushes over to the door and tries the handle; it doesn't open.

"Why am I still here, why haven't you got someone to open it?" His back straightens. "I'm going to have a shower and get changed. When I'm done I expect for those doors to be open," he spits.

"Well, here's the thing. They can't come for a few more hours. Trust me, I've tried, but they'll be here as soon as they can." I try to keep the smile out of my voice. Someone will certainly be coming, but it definitely isn't a locksmith.

"Just sort it and get me the fuck out of here." He turns his back and walks toward the shower grumbling.

"Sure thing, boss."

Turning the mic off, I can't believe how he accepted that. Maybe he really is losing it. Or he's playing me like I'm playing him. Only time will tell.

I raise my head toward the door when I hear a knock. "Come in."

Marco pushes through the door, a smile on his face. "Your guests have arrived, they're pulling up the driveway now."

"Perfect." Rising out of my seat, I grab the black silk tie from my desk and wrap it around my neck. "How does it look?"

"Very smart." I look at Marco and he's looking like a proud father. I don't think he's ever seen me fully sober.

Nodding at him, I walk past, doing up the button of my black Armani suit. It fits like a fucking glove. Heading over to the front door, I glance at my reflection in the mirror, rubbing my hand over my freshly shaven face. My eyes look sharp for the first time in years; they look alive.

Opening the door, I stand with my hands in my slacks, waiting for them to exit the black Escalades they've arrived in. I'm not sure which of the three Jax is in; all of the windows are blacked out.

The middle door opens and a man who I know is Jax from the image I've seen gets out.

He strides toward me. He too has chosen to dress in all black, his suit tailored to perfection. His blue eyes never leaving mine, his tall frame matches my own as he reaches me. He smiles fully and raises his hand to shake mine.

"Reed, I take it. Nice to meet you." He didn't wait for my response so I can only assume he has already seen an image of me too.

"Jax," I acknowledge him and take his hand in my returning his gesture.

"Come through to my office, we can go over the details in there," I tell him as I turn and walk back to my office. I can hear the tapping of his shoes and only his, so I am guessing he came in alone.

"Take a seat." Gesturing to the one opposite me, his eyebrows furrow but he opens his jacket button and sits. His right ankle sits on top of his left knee while his arms spread along the arms of the chair.

"Where's Carlos?" I can hear his agitation.

"You'll want to see this." I spin the monitor round and click the buttons. "You can watch the last couple of weeks on here and see how our friend is doing." My lips rise at my own joke.

"Look, I want to make the son of a bitch suffer. Trust me,

after what that cocksucker did to Caitlin he deserves it, but I don't have days to be here." Clearing his throat, he looks at the screen, and the anger is plain to see on his face.

"Where is Caitlin? I was hoping she'd be with you." I pause the videos to get his attention.

"She's here. I wanted to come in first, make sure everything was good." He stands and runs his hands through his hair. "She wants to put a bullet through his head herself." He sighs and looks out the window toward the guest house.

He taps on his phone and moments later there's a gentle tap on the door. I see the face I haven't seen for years, only she's all grown up and is now a beautiful woman.

"Fuck, Caitlin." I can't speak. Tears build in my eyes but now isn't the time.

"Reed, oh god! I've missed you so much." She rushes over and hugs me tightly. "I have tried looking for you for years."

"I'm sorry, Caitlin, I have let you down and I want to make up for it. We're family." I squeeze her back, pressing a kiss to her head.

She looks up, smiling at me. "It's all in the past. Now we move on. Now we can both truly be happy."

"Do you have a plan?" Jax questions, moving forward, reaching for Caitlin and pulling her under his arm. I try to keep the smile from my lips as I can only imagine how I would feel if someone hugged Maghan like that.

Laughing, I move back toward the desk to collect the key fob for the collar. "The only plan I have is that when we leave that house, he is dead at the end of it."

"Sounds like a good enough plan to me. I have a few things I brought with me. I'll grab them then I'm ready to go." He smiles at me but this one doesn't reach his eyes; it's quite disturbing.

"Let's see if there are any other wicked secrets he's been hiding," I say, smiling at him. "Let's go."

CHAPTER 21

Reed

Making our way to the guest house, Jax is dragging a metal carry on behind him. The wheels click over the paving slabs, almost the sound of dread. I smile to myself, thinking of the *Jaws* theme tune as he continues his decent down to the house, and I'm intrigued to see what he has with him.

"You ready? I am going to go in first, I want you to be a surprise," I tell Jax.

"Oh, I'll be a surprise. I can't fucking wait." His tone is serious; all jokes we had earlier are gone. He's rubbing his hands together, eager to get inside.

Pulling my shoulders back, I inhale. This is it, now is the time I can finally ruin this motherfucker!

I tap on the door. "Boss, I should be able to access the door now."

"About fucking time, what took them so fucking long," he spits. He continues mumbling to himself as I open the door and

"What the fuck is this?" He points to his neck and starts to pull on the choker that's locked in place.

"I don't know what kinky shit you're into, boss, that's your business." I chuckle as I close the door and move closer to him "Why don't we sit? I have some things we need to go over." Moving my head, I gesture toward a chair.

"I'm not staying in here. We can talk in the office. I need to make some calls. I also need to locate that whore so I can get this off of my fucking neck." He makes his way past me, but I grab his arm just as he's at my side.

"That wasn't a request," I say gruffly.

He laughs at me. "You're not in charge here, Reed. I'm the fucking boss. This may be your turf when I'm not around, but you need to remember who the fuck you're talking to." Yanking his arm away from me, he goes to exit the door.

I pull the fob from my pocket. "You sure you want to play it that way?" Turning to face him, I raise my brow in question.

"Watch it, Reed, you're treading in dangerous waters." He points his finger directly at me.

"Exactly where I want to be." Smiling at him, I press the button and his hand flies to his neck as his knees buckle beneath him and he falls to the floor screaming out, "What the fuck was that?"

"I'm starting to wade into deep water, Carlos. It's sink or swim for both of us, and I have a feeling that you're the only one of us that's going to fucking sink." Pressing the button again, I watch as he squirms around the floor, spittle flying from his mouth as he claws at his neck, opening the old wounds. It's funny; old wounds are exactly what we're here for.

I drag him toward the chair, leaving him lying on the floor while I go to the picture of stormy seas with a shipwrecked boat hanging on the wall. Pressing the side, it swings open, revealing a safe. I insert the code and retrieve some bits that I'll be needing.

I use the rope from the safe and secure him to the chair. Each leg is secured to a chair leg with his arms tied to the back of the chair behind his back.

Slapping his face, I get his attention. "It appears we have some things to speak about, Carlos."

"Fuck you," he hisses.

"That's not the right attitude, is it? I think you know why you're here, in this position, and a fuck you isn't going to cut it." I walk back and sit on the edge of the bed, facing him.

"What do you want?" He looks at me, struggling with his ties, the rope ripping his wrists and causing his skin to break.

"The truth." I lean forward, placing my elbows on my knees.

"About what? I don't know what you're talking about." His brows raise to the top of his head, a bead of sweat drops down the side of his face, and I can see he's worried but he'll try to hide it, putting a front on his fear.

"Okay, well, let's start with Maghan. Why did you tell me she committed suicide?" My jaw clenches at the thought of it.

"She was a distraction, one you didn't need. It was easy to send her away to a boarding school." He believes his own lies.

"Where is she now?" I look directly at him, waiting to see what he says.

"She finished and didn't say where she was going. The last we knew, she was headed for the UK." I quirk my brow up as the lies fall easily from his lips.

"Your parents, their death?" I watch as his jaw ticks.

"I'm still out for blood on that. I believe the Riveria Mafia were in on that but still can't prove it." His eyes shift, escaping mine.

"You don't think it was your father's other son?" I question.

Got him; his eyes bug and he starts to stutter. "He doesn't have another son, I'm his only son."

"That's where you're wrong, and you know it." Standing, I walk over to him and punch him in the face, feeling the crunch of bones breaking, and the splatter of blood from his nose sprays on my shirt.

"Now that was for the lies, but don't worry—you will pay for your sins." I smile as I walk toward the door.

"Maghan is alive and well, we know you killed your parents, and that I am the oldest son of our father, which means *I* am the don of the Russo mafia." His face is getting redder as he screams and shouts at me. "The time for talking with me is over, Carlos. You have apologies left to make and that's it… but not only to me." I open the door. "I think you should welcome one of our guests."

"Apologize, apologize for what? Everything I have done has been for the sake of this fucking family. I have sacrificed everything. Our father had no fucking back bone, he was happy with all he had. To prosper you need to take what should be yours, I did everything I had to do to survive." Panting, he looks at me, his eyes wide. I can see the anger in his face.

I laugh at him because I find it difficult to keep myself in check. "I.. I…I, that's all I'm hearing. Carlos, you've never cared about anyone else. You tried to cover your tracks, and the only reason it's taken this long was because my nose was full of coke for the past ten years." I rest my hand on the door handle as I tell him, "Our father was a good man, strong, successful, and got things done under the radar. Traits that you've never had."

Turning the handle, I look at Jax and nod my head, gesturing for him to enter.

He strolls in with a big grin on his face. "Good afternoon, Carlos. It's a pleasure to see you like this."

CHAPTER 22

Reed

I smirk when I watch how Carlos reacts to Jax's entrance. I know for certain he was not who he was expecting to see today, but I love to surprise people, and judging by the look on his face, I have excelled.

His Adam's apple bobs as he swallows loudly. He's starting to crack. I must admit the ease with which Jax is walking around the guesthouse is imposing.

Jax pulls his case and lifts it onto the bed, flipping it open with two clicks, his white teeth showing in a sinister smile when he takes in the contents.

"You don't happen to have a speaker, do you? I don't appear to have packed mine." His brows narrow and a frown fills his face.

"Err, sure." Heading over to the lounge room, I pick the speaker up and take it over to him. Of all the things he could have asked me for, a speaker is not what I would have expected. This guy is a mystery.

He stands, fiddling with his phone. My guess is he is trying to connect to the speaker, but he turns, lifts the speaker and places it on the kitchen island, and looks Carlos directly in the eye. "You owe your sister an apology."

"That useless cunt won't get anything from me." He sneers, spitting in Jax's direction.

"Excellent. I'm glad we know where we both stand, or sit in your case." Jax chuckles darkly.

"Reed, could you pass me some pliers?" His hand comes up, palm up outstretched toward me, but his eyes never leave Carlos.

Looking in his case, I smirk. I am impressed at his travel torture devices. I'm hoping that we can use these to make Carlos feel what we've felt over the years, make him pay for what he has done.

Passing him the pliers, I stand back, watching what's about to unfold and waiting for my turn.

Jax has taken his jacket off and stands twirling the pliers in front of Carlos, messing with his mind. A few minutes pass and he walks away and places the pliers down next to the speaker, undoing his tie and throwing it onto the bed.

He retrieves his phone and scrolls until music fills the room, only very lightly; I couldn't tell you what it is but it's classical and chilling.

"You can't beat classical music when you're unwinding, don't you agree, Reed?" Jax looks over to me with a smile.

"Absolutely," I agree and walk over to Carlos and take his head in my hands.

"It's clear we're not getting any answers from him, nor any apologies, and we know the truth. I know the end result here, but I also want to make him pay." I look at Jax, my expression stony.

"I understand," is all Jax says before he moves to his case and pulls out plastic sheeting. "I need help putting this across the floor."

Once we have the sheets over the floor, we lift Carlos up on the chair and place him in the center and stand back.

We bend down behind him and take each take a finger on the opposite hand and break them one by one. The crack of the bones are still heard over the music that's still playing softly. The screams from Carlos are blood curdling.

"You are quite noisy, Carlos, especially for someone that hasn't got anything to say," I tell him, my voice a rumble in his ear.

"You are never going to get away with this, my men will fucking kill you for this," he shouts.

"My men, not yours, and my men will be taking out the trash when we're finished." My thumb and forefinger grip his cheeks so hard they hollow inward.

"I was going to use these," Jax states holding the pliers I gave him, "but I don't feel we're quite ready for them yet." He tosses them back to the bed and reaches in his case, pulling out a hood and a whip.

I arch my brow at him and he holds a finger up to me.

"You know what's going to happen next, don't you? You know what happened to Caitlin under your say so." Jax slaps Carlos across the face. "Answer me."

"She was a useless cunt, never good at anything," he pants, pulling his wrists, still hoping he'll get free. Any hope of that just left, *not that he had any,* but the look in Jax's eyes is pure rage. His eyes are so black there is no return for Carlos.

Jax covers his head with the hood, stands back, and lets loose. Lash after lash lands on his legs and torso. You can hear the whoosh before the bite. I stand, watching as the whip opens Carlos's skin, ripping his white shirt, covering it in his blood, some sticking to the whip.

Finally Jax drops the whip after his rant. He needed this, and I'm happy he had it. This is about ridding us all of the past.

The hood covering his head is being pulled in to his mouth each time he breathes in deeply, in and out, in and out. It's getting wet with his saliva and he breathes quicker with panic.

Jax smiles at me as he reaches for his ankle, pulls out a knife, takes a stride toward Carlos, and stabs him in his side.

The scream of pain leaves him as his blood marks his shirt.

Jax withdraws the knife slowly, watching his blood ooze out. He stands back, reaches for the hood, smiles at Carlos, and says, "What goes around comes around, motherfucker."

"When I leave here, I'm going to kill you both," he pants.

"I think the loss of blood has gone to your head." I chuckle.

"Jax, I trust you're happy." I raise my brow.

"With the time we have, yeah." His head nods.

"Can you hold his head tight?" I walk over to Jax's case to see if I can find what I'm looking for and bingo! I go toward Carlos and stop.

"Right, hold his head," I say, gesturing toward Carlos.

"Open wide," I tell him, but he keeps his mouth closed. I talk in his ear about all the things we did together as children, everything we promised each other, then everything he did to ruin it.

"Stand behind him and squeeze his nose," I order Jax. I look at him as he changes his position. He stands behind him, holding him in a choke hold, his free hand squeezing his nose. His face is getting redder and redder, snot flying from his nose, until he finally gives up and opens his mouth.

Pulling the open mouth gag out of my back pocket, I slip it in his mouth and strap it up at the back of his head and nod at my handy work.

"I don't want you biting me," I say with a wink as I look at Jax, motioning him to get hold of his head again.

The knife I found in the case will be perfect. "I am doing this because of the wicked lies you told." He struggles against Jax's grip, spittle dripping from the gag down his chin.

Reaching across, I pick up the discarded pliers and lean forward. The pliers grip his tongue and that's when the first tears fall from his eyes.

Pulling his tongue out further, I slice across, hearing his scream followed by the gurgling sound of the blood quickly filling his mouth. Jax releases his head and he drops his head forward.

It's a sea of red, his blood pouring to the mat.

"Can we call Caitlin in now?" Jax looks at me. He is waiting for my response. He poses it like a question, but I know it isn't. However I nod, and he takes his phone out and starts typing, but she enters before he hits send.

"I take it you've been watching all this from outside. What did I tell you about waiting inside before you come out?" Jax tells her. "We wanted to know if you want him to bleed out or do you want the pleasure of ending him now?"

She thinks about it, I can tell. However she soon decides that it's much better for him to suffer than to end his life quickly.

Watching his life leave him makes me feel more alive than ever before.

CHAPTER 23

Reed

Watching Caitlin as she walks around her brother, I thought she would shy away but she has fire in her eyes that makes her look as deranged as Jax. She slaps her brother around his head, and he makes a gurgling sound. "Look at me," she tells him calmly.

Inhaling deeply, a huge smile takes over her face, making her brown eyes glow brightly. It makes me happy to be a part of this, and it makes me feel a little better to be able to give her this after how little I've done for her all this time.

"You know you're finished, Carlos. I am going to sit here and watch you take your last breath. You know you underestimated me for all those years, all those failed attempts to marry me off failed because I made it so. You were just too blind to see how I outsmarted you every time." She tuts at him and drops down on the end of the bed.

He goes to say something but only manages a murmur, and blood pours from his mouth, making her laugh. "What's the matter, lost your tongue?"

It turns out Carlos doesn't last as long as we expected. He takes his last breath, and the tears drop from Caitlin's eyes. At first we worry but then we realize these are tears of joy over the fact she is now free and can live her life as she wishes; well, as much as she can when she lives with a mafia Don.

We head inside and go straight to my office, and I gesture for them both to sit. Making my way to get some glasses, I pour each of us a drink to raise a glass to celebrate the ties that we've cut loose.

"To the demise of one sleazy son of a bitch, no more wicked secrets." I raise my glass, and the clink of the glasses rings throughout the room.

I press the button on the screen and see that Maghan is curled up reading a book, but I call through and her face breaks into a smile. "Baby, come to my office." She practically jumps from her seat.

"What, really?" She looks confused but tugs on her bottom lip.

My cock twitches at the sight and she makes her way to the door as I tell her, "Really."

"Since I learned about what he was up to, I set the wheels in motion to prevent these people from moving forward to the destinations they were supposed to be going, and now that I am Don, I will stop this entirely. The only thing we use the containers for will be the same as what was originally agreed upon when Carlos Senior was present. We need nothing more than what we have the market on. Our side is covered and our contacts are happy with the supply we have set up," I tell Jax confidently.

"I see no reason why we can't work together and build an alliance that can benefit us both." I tilt my head and look at him, waiting for his reaction.

"Do you plan to return to New York?" is his response.

"Honestly, no, I will return only to check on the remaining men we have. The ones I will send to New York are the ones I trust here. I'll let them run things on that end and liaise with our couriers," I tell him. "Sawyer has been keeping an eye on them all so I know who I can trust."

"I think we can agree to that, we can be beneficial to each other." He stands and puts his hand out for me to shake. "I think that'll be all. I would like to have stayed for longer but we have to get back, I have business to attend to." He nods his head. "I appreciate you reaching out and including us, I won't forget it."

The tap on the door interrupts us and we drop our hands. Jax reaches for Caitlin and furrows his brow as he looks between me and the door.

"It's okay, I have someone I'd like Caitlin to meet before you leave." I move over to the door and open it, and the weight I didn't know I had on my shoulders lifts when I see her standing there. Each and every time I look at her, I can't believe how much she's changed me, changed how I want my life to be.

Leaning down, I kiss her soft, pillowy lips gently and take her hand in mine, pulling her in to the office. We pass both Caitlin and Jax, and I gesture for them to sit back down.

I sit and pull Maghan to my lap. "Caitlin, this is Maghan." I smile as I see her mouth drop open.

"Maghan, as in your sister Maghan?" Her brow raises and she looks to Jax as if she needs confirmation.

"Step-sister, actually, but yes, that Maghan." I smile and pull her close as I inhale her citrusy scent.

She recovers quickly, I give her that, as she gets up and moves over to us and pulls Maghan in to a hug.

"Oh, my god, I am so happy to finally meet you. I am so sorry for everything you've been through," she says, still holding her in a tight grip.

Maghan laughs. "Erm, thanks, but Reed is helping me get through it. One thing I know for sure, if I wasn't running from your brother I wouldn't have found the true love of my life." She lifts her head and kisses me, and my heart beats quickly. If they weren't here I would have her on this desk. It feels like it's been too long since I sank in to her tight little pussy.

I have a feeling Jax knows this all too well when he stands. "Caitlin, we will see them when they visit New York. I think we all need time to adjust." He winks at me, and I know what he means. My cock is aching to be released and I can feel it pressing against my zipper, and having Maghan moving about in my lap is not helping.

Sliding her off my lap, I stand and shake Jax's hand. "I look forward to working with you," I tell him. Reaching for Caitlin, I hug her briefly goodbye and hear the rumble that Jax makes. I go to chuckle at that until I see him reach for Maghan, and red hot rage burns through me.

He looks over the top of her head and smirks at me. That cheeky motherfucker knew what he was doing so I just raise my head in acceptance. He has me there!

They take off out of the room, and I watch them leave through the front entrance and get into the waiting Escalades.

It's finally fucking over.

CHAPTER 24
Maghan

I follow him out the office as Jax and Caitlin leave. It was crazy seeing them here, but what was odd yet strangely comforting was that they each had blood splatters over their clothes, yet they spoke to each other as if it didn't exist.

The lightness I feel inside is indescribable, but I have to know for sure that he's gone. "He's dead... right?" I peer up at Reed and he smiles at me.

"Yes, he is. He won't be coming after you any more, sugar, it's over." His hand snakes around the back of my neck as he pulls me toward his hard chest.

"I have to see him," I blurt out. It's not that I don't believe him, but I feel the need to see his corpse.

"It's not a pretty sight. My men haven't been to clean the room yet," he tells me, pulling back slightly, his eyes squinting. I can tell he's seeing if he thinks I'm ready.

"I need this, Reed, it's the closure I've been looking for," I say as my hands grip at his shirt.

"Fine." He swallows loudly and his Adam's apple moves up and down. A soft moan escapes me, and he chuckles and reaches for my hand. "Come on, the quicker we get there the quicker we get back." He winks at me, and god! From that look alone, my panties dampen.

We get to the end of the garden and we're standing facing the door. I feel him squeeze my hand. "You don't have to do this, sugar. He's gone; you don't have anything to prove to him."

"I want to, I want to see it for myself," I say, stepping forward and opening the door. I see the blood-soaked mat on the floor. Carlos is tied to the chair and he looks a fucking mess, but there is no denying that the son of a bitch is dead.

I walk over to him and push him to see if there's any reaction, but nothing. His body slumps to the side. I tilt my head and screw my face as I move slightly closer to him. "Fuck, you cut his tongue out." I turn to look at Reed who's standing with his arms crossed, looking really fucking pleased with himself.

"It appears that way," is all he says as he moves and sits on the bed that has a variety of weapons strewn about on the messy linen.

"Happy now you've seen for yourself?" He smiles.

"Yep," I say as I walk over to him. Reaching out, I run my hand across the side of his face and into his thick hair and squeeze tightly as I lean in to kiss him.

"Let's head back up." He goes to pull away, and I smile, shaking my head no as I stand back and pull the t-shirt I am wearing over my head.

"I need you to fuck me," I tell him as I let my hands push down the shorts from my hips, taking down the panties I was wearing. I don't have time to do a strip tease right now, I need him and I need him now.

His eyes darken as he takes me in; he traces me from head to toe. "So let me get this straight, sugar, you want me to fuck you in front of a fucking corpse."

Chuckling, I walk over to him as he frees his cock from his slacks, licking my lips when I see his tip glistening with precum. "Oh, yes. I think you've read the room pretty well." I straddle his lap and feel the silky softness of his cock pressing against my pussy lips which makes me groan.

I lean backward and rip at his shirt, pulling him free from it, hearing the tiny buttons clatter across the floor. My hand presses against his chest so he is flush against the bed, and I shimmy my way up his body.

I tease him with my pussy, my lips touching his chin, when he grabs my hips and sits me on his face and feasts on me like I'm his last fucking meal.

Licking, nipping, and sucking, the sopping noises I can hear drive me wild. One hand grips his head, pulling him closer, as I gyrate against his face, taking everything I can from him. The other hand reaches for my breast, teasing and pulling. I'm getting so close, and my pants turn into moans.

"Fuck, Reed, I..I'm so fucking close," I tell him.

He hums in acknowledgment which only pushing me further. My legs still and start to shake.

"Oh God, fuuuuck," I scream as I come all over his face.

He gently pushes me back so I'm flat against the bed and looks down at me, my juices covering his mouth. "Not God, sugar, just me." He winks.

I roll my eyes and chuckle, but he cuts it off as his mouth lands on mine. "You taste so fucking good, sugar." I hum against his lips and yelp as his cock thrusts into me without notice. "Fuck, you're like a fucking vice." His lips roam over my neck and shoulder as he gives me a moment to adjust.

"Fuck me, Reed, please," I beg. By now I don't care how fucking needy I sound. When it feels this good having his cock buried inside me, I would get on my hands and knees and beg. I won't tell him that though.

The sounds of our skin slapping against each other is loud as, pound after pound, he thrusts into me, never letting up. It feels like seconds since I last came but I can feel the sensations building the harder and faster he goes. My legs start to shake as I reach the point that I couldn't return from even if I wanted to.

I call his name and feel myself clench around his cock over and over. He follows and roars his release, filling me with his warm seed.

He looks between us as he slides his cock free and watches as his cum drips out of my pussy. He gathers it up and pushes it back in. He keeps his fingers inside as he reaches up the bed and kisses me softly.

"Mine, sugar, forever."

EPILOGUE

Reed

One year later…

I'm sitting on the patio overlooking the ocean. I see the waves gently move back and forth as the sun rises from beyond. I love this time of the morning; it's peaceful and gives me time to think.

The smile fills my face when I hear the familiar sound that's been filling our villa recently. For someone so tiny, he has lungs the size of the ocean I am looking at, that's for sure.

I stand as the cries bellow out and don't let up. I head back inside, making my way back to our room. Maghan is standing, rocking little Massimo, and they look like a vision. "He's hungry and he just couldn't wait one moment while I went for a pee." She sighs.

She's so good with him. He's the most precious thing I've ever seen, and demanding. "I wonder where he gets his impatience from." I chuckle as I duck the pillow she throws at me. Lowering down, I pick it up and walk to the bed and sit down.

"He's perfect, you've given me the most precious gift I have ever received," I tell her.

"Listen, I appreciate that, but today I am cranky. He doesn't seem happy with anything I'm doing for him, and I don't know what else to do." Her palm meets her face and her shoulders sag.

"Sugar, you're tired. He keeps the whole villa up at night, probably the whole town. You're doing everything perfectly. How about you leave him with me and rest for a while, maybe go into town." I smile. Walking over to her, I take Massimo from her and place a kiss on her head.

If Marco has plans, he doesn't have anymore. Without Maghan, I don't have the first clue what I am doing, but I am not telling her that. She needs the rest.

"We will see you later," I tell her confidently as I leave the room and head to my office.

Massimo is in his basket and his rattle shakes back and forth as I work on the remaining shipments we have coming through. Everything has gone back to how it was before Carlos decided he wanted to fuck it up, so it's smooth sailing as they say, no pun intended.

An hour goes by and Maghan walks in, looking as radiant as ever. "How's he been?" Picking him up, she inspects him. I won't take offence by it; if I were her I would probably do the same.

"He's been good. We've been working on the boats, haven't we, little guy." I look at him, and he moves his arm and hits Maghan in the face with his rattle.

"I thought you were going out. What's it been, an hour?" I raise my brow.

"Well, I popped out quickly, came home and showered, but I missed him too much." She looks down, her cheeks heating.

"Just him, huh?" I laugh.

"Well, not just him, buuut…" She laughs, coming over to kiss me, all PG as the little guy's around. She doesn't want him seeing anything rude. I mean, she will fuck in front of a corpse but not a sleeping baby.

"Are you busy right now?" Her voice is quiet and her eyes are roaming the room, looking anywhere but at me.

"I don't have to be, what's wrong?" I tell her, moving my head to catch her eye line.

"I need to talk to you about something, but if you're busy then I can come back later," she says quickly and goes to leave the room.

"Hold up, sugar," I say, walking to the door to stop her from leaving.

"Go take a seat, tell me what's on your mind." I sit in the chair next to her, and she leans over and places Massimo back into his basket.

"Okay, well I found something out today. I should have probably told you earlier, but I wasn't sure." She starts rambling and I'm not following.

"Wait, if you only found out today how could you have told me before?" I ask. "Sugar. You don't have to be worried about telling me anything, I promise." I take her hands in mine, squeezing gently.

"I'm pregnant." Her eyes meet mine and she starts to chew on her bottom lip nervously. If she carries on she won't have a lip left, the way she's gnawing at it.

I laugh. "Oh, sugar, I'm so fucking happy."

She releases a breath. "You are?"

"Yes. I want everything with you, and one thing I'll never tire of is seeing you grow with my children." I take her in my arms and hug her tightly.

As much as I despise Carlos, his wicked secrets changed my life. Maybe later than they should have done, but I'm one lucky son of a bitch. What I have here in my arms is something greater than I could have ever imagined I would have.

Only one person is smiling here, and it ain't Carlos fucking Russo.

Wicked Secrets

The End

Acknowledgments

I have loved writing this duet and although they have taken a while to get completed, I am so happy that I decided to go through with getting these beauties out there, however, none of this would be possible without those close to me who offer their support and guidance.

My husband as always, my rock and my world, who supports me and my love of all things books.

Phil, for stepping in to help me when I needed it most! I am so grateful for you taking all that time, I can't really put it in to words.

And my ARC Team, who are amazing and to everyone who has shared about this book, liked posts, it all means the world to me.

Lastly, If I didn't mention this I could get disowned and I am not sure that I would want that, but apparently Reed has been claimed by Penny… or has he…lol 😉

This has been a Wicked journey and one I hope you continue to take with me.

If you enjoyed this book, please consider leaving a review xx

About the Author

S.E.Robin is a new self published author of Mafia, Billionaire and the occasional MC romance novels, that all have a little dark steamy side to them.

I live in the UK with my Husband and love to read all types of genres.

Why not come follow me on the following social media platforms to find out what's next…

TIKTOK
INSTAGRAM
S.E Robin FACEBOOK PROFILE
S.E. Robin READER GROUP
THREADS

Printed in Dunstable, United Kingdom

64821048R00080